FORBIDDEN FRUIT

A NOVEL OF LUST AND DESIRE SATIATED

FORBIDDEN FRUIT

TERI LEE

Forbidden Fruit

Copyright © 2021 by Teri Lee. All rights reserved.

No part of this publication may be reproduced, stored in a retrieval system or transmitted in any way by any means, electronic, mechanical, photocopy, recording or otherwise without the prior permission of the author except as provided by USA copyright law.

The opinions expressed by the author are not necessarily those of URLink Print and Media.

1603 Capitol Ave., Suite 310 Cheyenne, Wyoming USA 82001
1-888-980-6523 | admin@urlinkpublishing.com

URLink Print and Media is committed to excellence in the publishing industry.

Book design copyright © 2021 by URLink Print and Media. All rights reserved.

Published in the United States of America

Library of Congress Control Number: 2021922092
ISBN 978-1-68486-012-8 (Paperback)
ISBN 978-1-68486-013-5 (Digital)

20.10.21

ABOUT THE AUTHOR

Teri Lee, age 29, was born in the British Crown Colony of Hong Kong and raised in America. She is the product of California's University System. Unmarried, she lives on the east side of the San Francisco Bay. This is her first novel.

Sorry, Ms. Lee does not grant interviews.

ACKNOWLEDGEMENT

Dear Maggie:

Wisdom, patience, and a sense of humor; you have it all in just the right amounts.

Thank you.

INTRODUCTION

Forbidden Fruit is a novelette of those amoral. It contains sex, bi-sex, tri-sex and more sex. There is no message, no social-redeeming value; it may be devoured in an evening. Forget your stress – turn your imagination loose – and enjoy a fantasy romp.

Just as all criminals are not sociopaths; all sociopaths are not criminals. CEOs, politicians, call girls, playboys, even some Presidents display sociopathic personalities; we are probably surrounded and exposed to more sociopaths than we will ever know.

'SOCIOPATHIC PERSONALITY: Differing in a sense of right and wrong from the average person. Notoriously amoral – an absence of, indifference towards, or disregard for moral beliefs. Low fear including stress-tolerance, toleration of unfamiliarity and danger, and high self-confidence and social assertiveness. Demand for immediate gratification, and poor behavioral restraints.' (*Source unknown.*)

PART ONE
Father Knows Best

Clarice Chan was beautiful beyond belief. A full head of thick luxurious hair cascaded over shoulders that framed her delicate Chinese face. Large, almond shaped eyes and high cheek-bones suggested hidden mysteries of the ethereal East. Her neck, a bit long, added to her magnetism, much like a young Audrey Hepburn. Seven years of ballet and charm school added grace and poise. Though she had just turned eighteen it annoyed her that she still had the lithe, athletic body of a fifteen-year-old. Her mother said she would always look much younger than she really was – it was an Asian-thing. Both parents were very protective of her; she had never been on date with a boy.

Her father, Tommy, was a successful real estate entrepreneur forming groups of Hong Kong investors that developed low-income rental property and strip malls. He was extroverted; moving comfortably in both Eastern and Western business environments. He loved golf, playing with a six handicap. Tommy always had a smile, a good joke, and a warm pat on the back to everyone he met. His successes attracted more; the money tree bore abundant fruit.

To suppliers and tradesmen, he was known as Ten-Percent-Tommy; demanding a tribute of ten percent of the gross from those who did business with him. Still, everyone was happy; the investors, the contractors, all had a share of the pie; Tommy made sure his was the biggest slice. America's ever-expanding economy more than kept up with his greed.

Allison, her still-beautiful mother, owned one of the largest travel agencies in Oakland's Chinatown. America's loosening of relations with China kept her booked solid conducting tours to Beijing and beyond. She enjoyed guiding young Chinese around the country of their ancestors. The trips were usually three weeks in length; she scheduled four a year. Tommy wanted her to sell the business and spend more time with him but she loved to travel and liked being independent. As was the custom in China she received kick-backs from all the airlines, the Chinese hotels, and merchants; life was good.

Tommy and Allison came from wealthy families in Hong Kong. They were married in 1963, when Allison became pregnant with Clarice. In 1967 Red Guards from the Mainland demonstrated in the British Colony causing riots; China rationed water to four days a week forcing residents to use their bathtubs as storage tanks. Tommy's father ordered his son to take his family to America where it was safe and fertile for business.

English was their second language. Adapting quickly to California's West Coast culture; with their Chinese work ethic and sense of business, success was a given. Clarice blended in effortlessly, making friends and picking up American patois while attending private schools. She had the best of everything. Tommy bought a luxurious house in Piedmont, a small community of millionaires across the bay from San Francisco that reflected his status as a player in the business world. Life was indeed very good for the two émigrés from Hong Kong.

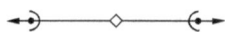

It was in late June; Allison had been gone seven days on a twenty-one-day excursion. Tommy told Clarice she would accompany him to Honolulu for a week. He had business to do and his daughter could work on getting a suntan. *I have the best father in the world*, she thought.

He was meeting with a group of local Chinese representing a Huie, (Chinese investment group) interested in buying into a block of apartments being built in Albany. They flew first class on United; Tommy had booked a water-view two-bedroom suite at the Kahala Hilton. Being from the Mainland, he rented a Mercedes; first impressions were very important.

"Clarice, you stay by the pool, I have to meet with some men downtown. Order lunch on your own, and don't stay in the sun too long; you'll burn."

"Yes Dad. When will you be back?"

"I don't know; I'll try to make it back for dinner. I'll call and leave word with the operator."

It was ten-thirty when Tommy drove off in the Mercedes and eleven when Clarice headed for the pool. The Hawaiian climate is deceiving. It's never too hot, there's always a pleasant breeze. Lying out by the pool Clarice felt relaxing warmth from the sun that was pure heaven. This being her first trip to the Islands she thought it paradise as the fireball slowly, surely, turned her pale porcelain skin pink. By two o'clock she realized she'd over-done it; her back itched. She got up to their suite just as the phone rang; it was her father.

"Hi honey, I may be a little late; I'm having dinner with some people. You order something from room service; I'll be back as soon as I can."

"Dad, I've got a sunburn; my back is on fire; my legs are sore."

"I told you not to lie out in the sun so long. Damn. Look, here's what you do; call Room Service and tell them you want a cup of vinegar from the kitchen. Then fill the bath tub with water as hot as you can stand it, pour the vinegar in with the hot water and soak for at least fifteen minutes. Then shower off. The vinegar will take away the pain."

"I'll smell like a salad."

"Not if you shower off and then rub down with some body lotion. I'll be back as soon as I can."

"Okay – bye."

"Bye."

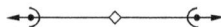

Tommy didn't get back until late. The bedside light in Clarice's bedroom was lit as he peeked in; she sleepily greeted him. "Hi Dad, how did it go?" Clarice pulled the sheet up around her shoulders; she wasn't wearing anything but a pair of panties due to the inflammation.

"Fine; I think Honolulu will be fertile ground to plow. There's a lot of money in this town that needs to be put to work. How do you feel?"

"Better, but I still itch…"

"I spoke to one of the investors and he recommended Aloe Vera oil that relieves the soreness. I bought a bottle on the way here; do you want to try it?"

"Sure, what do I do, drink it?"

"No silly; you rub it on. Here, roll over and I'll put some on your back."

Tommy opened the bottle, pouring a bit between her shoulder blades and began gently spreading it over her back. Lying on her stomach with her eyes closed Clarice loved the way her father touched her. His hands were soft, yet firm, as he slowly rubbed in circles over her shoulders and worked his way down to the small of her back. It felt good. Thoughts came to her – thoughts she couldn't believe she was thinking.

"Do my legs please; the back of the knees hurt."

Tommy poured some more oil on her legs, gently rubbing it in being careful not to cause any pain. He noticed a wetness in the crotch of her panties but ignored it as he heard her breath struggling. *She's growing up, he thought.*

"There, that's it; you can do your front, I'm going to turn in."

"Okay Dad. Thank you; it feels better."

"Good; see you in the morning for breakfast?"

"Sure, – goodnight."

"Goodnight." Tommy left the room, closing the door behind him.

Clarice rubbed some more of the lotion on the front of her legs before working up to her stomach and chest. Her hands softly rubbed the pleasant smelling oil on her breasts even though they had not been exposed to the sun; the lotion made her nipples stand up. With one hand slowly massaging a nipple she reached down with the other to delicately fondle herself through her panties. The orgasm was an explosion of lights and fire and gasps and throbs; she thought was going to die. The second one was milder, but just as good.

Curling around a pillow she slept a deep restful slumber until her Dad knocked firmly on the door; "Hey, are you going to sleep all day? It's eight-thirty, breakfast is being sent up. Get up sleepy head."

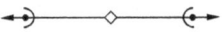

Clarice lathered suntan lotion all over her body before trying another hour by the pool. Her skin seemed to be going from pink to a light brown but still itched.

After a hot shower she went down to the lobby to explore the few shops in the hotel; she bought a full length silk Muumuu made in China. It was expensive but she knew her Dad wouldn't mind. It felt better on her body than the rougher clothes she'd packed. The rest of the day was spent watching TV and reading a book on Egyptian history she'd checked out of the Piedmont Public Library.

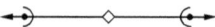

Tommy was having a field day; he'd received commitments of over five million dollars towards the Albany project. Several of the Hawaiian investors said they knew his Dad and had heard of what Tommy had done for the Hong Kong tongs. He was in solid with the Huie.

Calling Clarice, he apologized that he would not be back for dinner. "Honey, tomorrow I'll take you around the island. We'll spend all day together – just you and me – I promise."

"Okay Dad. I miss you; there's nothing but junk on the TV. Oh, I've got a surprise for you; I bought a dress."

"Good. Show it to me when I get back."

It was another late night for Tommy; he was obligated to have dinner and drinks to celebrate making the deal. He was tired when he let himself into the suite. Clarice was asleep on the couch; she was wearing the silk Muumuu and looked like a vision from heaven. For a moment Tommy hesitated; *what am I thinking? I must be crazy.*

Clarice stirred, slowly opening those beautiful eyes, "Hi Dad, I was reading and I guess I fell asleep." She stood up, smiling and with a slow pirouette exclaimed, "What do you think of the dress?"

"I think it's fantastic! It fits perfectly. Turnaround again, I want to see the back."

Clarice turned; the red silk had the pattern of a golden dragon woven into it that seemed to come alive as she pivoted.

"My God you are a beautiful young lady."

"It cost a lot of money…"

"Don't worry about it; it had your name on it."

Clarice came over and threw her arms around him giving him a big hug. "I'm glad you like it. I want to look good for you."

Pulling her arms from around his neck he said, "Honey, I've had a long day. Let's turn in. Tomorrow we're going to see some surfers and have lunch at a special place I was told about."

"Okay." Both headed off to their separate bedrooms.

"Dad?"

"What honey?"

"Dad, could you rub some of that Aloe Vera oil into my back? It feels good."

"Yes honey, let me get out of these street clothes and into some pajamas first."

The rubdown lasted a bit longer and was a bit slower than yesterday. Clarice was in heaven. Going off to his bedroom Tommy wished Allison would ask for a rubdown; she never asked for anything.

After breakfast, Tommy and Clarice drove off towards Koko Head, and Hanauma Bay where they stopped to survey that hidden Hawaiian delight. Both wore casual clothes and were in awe of the beautiful, perfectly shaped, bay surrounded by low hills. The beach was almost deserted so early in the morning.

"Look Dad, see the fish?"

"I do; it looks like a giant aquarium."

"Look over there; see the two people snorkeling? Could we come back her and snorkel too?"

"Yes, maybe tomorrow, if I can complete my business in time. Come on let's get back in the car. We've got a whole island to drive around."

The day was perfect; both had a wonderful time oohing and ahhing at the beauty of a tropical island so primitive, yet so modern. The two-lane road was easy driving as it wound around the coastline; the blue ocean on the right, mountains and palm trees on the left with a sprinkling of homes and small businesses scattered about. They lunched at the Mormon Polynesian Cultural Center and watched some Tahitian students do a sexy tamouré dance that excited both of them. Then it was off to view surfers riding the big breakers of Sunset Beach.

A bikini wearing brown-skinned young girl caught a big roller and started down the face of the monster wave; barely ahead of the breaking charging foam cascading behind her. "Dad, look at that one; how do they stay up on those little boards?"

"I don't know, but I don't think I want to try it."

"Me neither; you could get killed doing that."

The girl rode the roller until the pounding energy of the water dissipated, forcing her to dive off the board; then popping up to paddle out for another dare-devil ride. The surfers put on a show both fascinating and scary at the same time. Clarice and her Dad were amazed people would risk their lives to challenge giant waves just for the fun of it.

"Come on let's get going; the afternoon commuter traffic is going to be awful," Tommy said as he took her arm to lead her back to the car."

"Dad, this is the best day I think I've ever had. You are the best Daddy in the World," Clarice threw her arms around Tommy kissing him on the cheek."

"I'm glad you're having a good time."

"Super."

The commuter traffic was terrible; the freeway from Pearl City through Honolulu and out toward their hotel slowed to a ten mile per hour crawl. It was seven o'clock before they finally opened the door to their suite. "Yuk, how can they do it? How can people put up with so much congestion every day?" Clarice said as she headed over to get a bottle of water out of the fridge.

"It's what they have to put up with to live in paradise. Gasoline is the most expensive in America, the rents are high, the City is crowded beyond belief, but look at the climate; look at the where we drove – it is beautiful beyond belief."

"It is heaven if you have money like us."

"True; now get in the shower and we'll get ready for dinner."

"Okay, thanks for a great day. Can I wear my muumuu to dinner?"

"I had a great day too; wear it tomorrow, I'm planning something special."

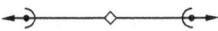

Both dined light on salad, seafood and rice. Tommy didn't normally drink wine or liquor. They split a small truffle dessert.

"I'm tired, what say we turn in early?" Tommy inquired as he signed for the dinner.

"Me too; no Telly or reading for me, I'm going to crash. That was a good albacore."

Up in the suite each headed for their separate bedrooms. Tommy had just put on his pajamas when Clarice called to him. "Daddy, could you rub my back?"

"Are you still sore?" he called back.

"No; but your back rubs feel good. The Aloe Vera oil smells good. I like it."

"Okay; I'm spoiling you rotten."

She was lying on her back on top of the sheets; wearing only her bikini panties. She was breathtakingly attractive Tommy thought as he picked up the bottle of lotion. "Roll over on your stomach, Princess."

He oiled and rubbed her ever so gently starting with her neck and shoulders then slowly massaging down her back and legs to her feet and toes. "Oh Daddy, it feels so good; could you do my neck again?"

"Sure honey," Tommy poured some more oil in his palm and as he moved up to her rub her neck she turned over; "Rub my front; do my boobs," she breathlessly spoke.

Tommy was somewhat stunned; this was his daughter – his little girl. Her small firm breasts were swelling and contracting with her breathing; the nipples were erect.

This is crazy, he thought; but he couldn't stop.

His palm full of liquid spilled onto her left breast as he began to slowly rub the orb and nipple, "There, is that better," he said.

"Oh yes Daddy, yes – it's so much better," she whispered, as she put her hand on top of his.

There was no hurry; Tommy was experienced and good at what he did. He took his time, always making sure Clarice was pleasured. It was a night that went on forever. The two of them came together, bonding naturally as though they were made in heaven for each other. Clarice had no idea anything could possibly be so good; she wanted him to never stop. Tommy knew he was committing a forbidden taboo, one that could send him to prison, but he didn't care. There was nothing in the world but his little Clarice and the ecstasy she gave him.

The next morning the only witness to the coupling was a bloody towel that was washed in the bathtub as they showered. Tommy was careful to muss up his bed and pound the pillow so the maid would not suspect a thing.

My God; what have I done? I am insane, he thought.

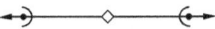

"I have a meeting at ten o'clock. Are you all right?"

"Yes Daddy, I'm more than all right; I'm super!"

"Clarice what we did last night was wrong; it is a sin for a father and daughter to fornicate."

Yes Daddy, but how can it be a sin when what we did last night was so good. I love you Daddy – I love you in every way..."

"Clarice – little one – Clarice, we cannot..."

"I read in my book the Egyptians did it; they fucked with the whole family."

"That was then; a long time ago... and don't use that word."

"Chinese emperors did it..."

"I know; but that was a long time ago too. Look, I have to go. You stay in the room today Get some rest and think about what happened. It was wrong."

"Yes Dad I will; can we go to Hanauma Bay this afternoon?"

Tommy couldn't believe what he was hearing; she didn't feel guilty, she didn't feel remorse. She was a teenager; she wanted to go snorkeling. "If I can get away early, we'll go snorkeling. Maybe the hotel will have some gear we can rent."

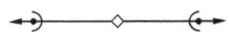

The meeting went well, Tommy had the ability to compartmentalize things in his mind; thoughts of Clarice didn't interfere. Everyone agreed on an interest bearing escrow with regular payments based upon progress or time. The Hawaiians knew they could trust him and knew he'd make them a lot of money even though he was getting the lion's share of the deal. A toast of hot tea was made and Tommy bowed out of dim-sum, saying he'd promised to take his daughter snorkeling. The Chinese businessmen respected him for putting his family first.

Getting back to the hotel Clarice had already picked up two sets of flippers, masks, and snorkels. "The pool life guard recommended these as being the best; the masks are smaller, to fit our faces. He gave me a lesson on how to use them – it's easy. I'll show you when we get to the bay. Oh, and I bought two grass mats to lie on."

She was wearing a new bikini bathing suit that fit her like a second skin. *God, she is exquisitely beautiful*, Tommy thought. "Where did you get that swimsuit?" he asked.

"At the hotel shop; do you like it?" she said smiling as she turned for his admiration.

Lightly he replied, "If your tan gets any darker you will look like a native. Pack some water; I'm going to change into my trunks and walking shorts. We'll stop and get some sandwiches on the way. Do you have anything to wear over your bikini?"

"I bought a Tahitian wraparound pāreu; it's what the locals wear."

"Okay, I'll be out in a minute," he said as he headed for his bedroom.

Every day in Hawaii is gorgeous and this day was no exception. Most of the locals were at work; the automobile traffic was light. Stopping at a fast-food Subway for sandwiches and chips, they declined sodas, preferring the water Clarice carried in her shoulder bag. Tommy enjoyed the drive as much as Clarice.

Being a weekday, Hanauma Bay was sparsely occupied. A just-right spot was vacant over by a rock formation jutting out into the bay.

"Dad, this is perfect. Come on, take your pants off, and I'll show you what I learned," she said as she unwrapped her pāreu, letting it fall carelessly onto the spread-out mat. Tommy carefully stepped out of his cut-offs, folding them before laying them on the mat adjacent to hers. Together they walked to the water's edge each carrying their diving gear.

"Dad, stick your foot in the water – it's warm. Oh, this is going to be fun. Here follow me." She bent over and splashed water onto her mask before spitting on the glass. Looking up she said, "You gotta do that to keep the mask from fogging up. It looks icky, but it's not."

Clarice went on to explain to her father how it was easier to put on the flippers when you were near waist deep as your body would provide flotation, making it less awkward to walk. She demonstrated how to float face down and breathe through the snorkel; and how to clear it in case water splashed in. They both agreed not to go out deeper than Clarice's chest high.

The water was calm and clear and loaded with all manner of small tropical fish. Everywhere they turned to look little exotically colored fish, coral rocks and swaying seaweed dazzled their eyes. Clarice took a deep breath, diving to swim along the bottom beside a small school of black spotted yellow fish that scattered at her approach. Tommy remained floating on the surface looking through his mask in the crystal-clear water he followed every graceful maneuver she performed. The swimsuit did accent her young body; he was getting an erection in spite of himself.

Clarice surfaced a few yards away, before taking another breath and diving down to swim back. Breaking the water in front of him she spit out her snorkel and lifted her mask to her forehead. With a mischievous smile she said in a low voice. "Daddy, something's peeking out of the top of your trunks, do you want some help to putting it back in?"

Embarrassed, he dodged her reaching hand, "I don't need any help – it's the water – it's the… I don't know what it is. Come on let's go in and get a sandwich."

"Can you walk out of the water like that?"

"I can if you leave me alone."

She laughed and waded out ahead of him.

Where did she come from? Who is she? She can't be my daughter, he thought as he slowly followed her, willing the swelling to go down. *But she is, oh God.*

They finished their sandwiches before taking a stroll down the beach. "Isn't this a fantastic place? Clarice commented.

Agreeing, Tommy added, "It is striking, the perfect beach; but I'll bet it's crowded on the weekends."

"Let's head back and go in one more time."

"Okay, but I don't want to get a sunburn."

"You won't, I'll put suntan lotion on your back, come on," she started to run.

"I'm coming."

On the drive home both itched from sand, sweat, and salt. The car's air conditioning helped to ease the discomfort. Traffic had picked up, but most of it was headed in the opposite direction.

"Clarice, honey, we've got to talk."

"Sure Dad…"

"Don't interrupt; you must listen and understand. I love you like a father. What happened the last couple of days is not as a father. What we've done is legally wrong and against the rules of society. It is forbidden fruit that we have tasted. Don't you see?"

FORBIDDEN FRUIT

"I see dad, but didn't Eve eat the apple?"

"Given to her by the serpent; an agent for the Devil. Not only could I go to jail, your mother would hate us, all our friends, yours and mine, would ostracize us. It is a lose-lose situation. We must stop."

"Dad, could I say something?"

"What?"

"I know what we did was bad, however, I also know many daughters fall in love with their fathers…"

"Nevertheless, it is not acted on."

"That's true, still they do and I'll bet some act on it like we did."

"Perhaps, but dammed few."

"I don't want to hurt Mom and I don't want anyone to find out. At home I'll be your daughter and love you as a father. Anyway, I can't help but think we must have known each other in another time, another place. God has played a trick on us; bringing us back together as father and daughter when in the past we were lovers."

True, she doesn't resemble Allison or me, could it be? "That's reincarnation B.S. It doesn't happen except in those books you read. It is a fiction; there is no scientific proof…"

"There's no proof it doesn't happen, aren't we all related through DNA?"

"We'd be leading two lives…"

"We're Chinese and American leading two different lives already. We eat Chinese at home, American in restaurants; our friends are Chinese, and Guai-lo, (Chinese, for a Caucasian). You do business with Chinese and Americans, treating them differently, following different rules and customs for each. Why can't we do the same?"

Tommy braked for a red light. *Arguing with a teenager, is impossible,* Tommy thought. "Okay let's change the subject daughter; what do you want for dinner tonight, Steak or Chinese?"

"Steak – can I wear my Muumuu?"

"I'll make reservations at the Canoe Club; one of my investors is a member."

The drive to the hotel continued with each of them silent in their thoughts.

Back in their room Tommy called Room Service for a cup of Vinegar; twenty minutes in a hot tub would relieve his pain. Clarice's burn had morphed into a golden brown.

Tommy dressed in white slacks and a loose silk Hawaiian print shirt looking very much the local, except for the red nose. Clarice was stunning in her fierce dragon Muumuu. As they started out the door Tommy asked, "Do you have anything on under that dress?"

"Perfume and panties," she saucily answered.

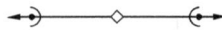

"Daddy, you are the best-looking man here."

"And, you the most beautiful."

Shrimp cocktail, superbly grilled, medium-rare, New York steak, baked potato with all the trimmings, and a chocolate mousse dessert ended a perfect day.

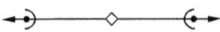

"Honey – can you come in here and rub some of that Aloe Vera oil on my back? I itch all over." Tommy was between the sheets in his boxer shorts. The vinegar soak had removed the soreness, but not the dry, burnt, skin.

"Just a minute; I'll be right in." She entered with the bottle of lotion wearing her Tahitian pâreu; she was naked underneath. Tommy was lying face down on the bottom sheet; the rest of the covers were pulled back to the foot of the bed. Pouring some solution in her palm before rubbing them together, she spread the fragrant oil over his shoulders massaging slowly in circles. "Does that feel better?"

"Very good, thank you."

Clarice oiled his legs being careful not to get too close to any of his private parts. She went back up to his neck before asking him to turn over. He protested; he could do the front himself. Her insistence made him comply.

She poured more of the moisturizer out of the bottle on his chest and began rubbing his pectoral muscles working her hands to his nipples. Her fingers gently pinched the erect little buttons, making him sigh and breathe deeper.

She's driving me out of my mind; there's electricity in her touch. Aiee-ya – Aiee-YA!! "That feels good; where did you learn to do it?"

"I sometimes do it to myself; do you like it?" she replied as she continued to slowly rub in a circular motion teasing his tiny titties.

"Very much, don't stop – Aiee-ya."

She bent down to gently nibble on the left nipple.

"Oh – oh God – don't stop. I do love it." His chest was heaving; his hand had gone to the top of her head pushing down forcing her lips harder on his little button.

The sex was better than ever. When both were satiated Tommy put his arm around her as she rested her head on his chest, "Clarice love, we are on a path that most-certainly cannot end well. But since we've both elected to go down this off-limits road I might as well teach you some skills that will enhance the pleasure for both of us."

"Are these things you do with Mother?"

"No, your Mother is very conservative; we only do it Missionary style; I don't think she likes sex."

"Why did you marry then?"

"It was arranged by our families – I hardly knew her"

"That sounds awful. Where did you learn these things you're going to teach me?"

"I travel to Hong Kong a lot; there were companions who taught me."

"Were they prostitutes?"

"Not like you think of them here in America; they are ladies of pleasure that are available on a high level. Often, they're dinner companions at social business affairs. Hong Kong is different than America."

"I see I think – don't you ever worry you'll catch a disease?"

"No, these ladies are disease-free; they are the cream of the crop."

"I never knew there were women like that."

"Kitten, there are lots of things you don't know. I will teach all I know; I want you to know the pleasure that can be had between a man and a woman."

"Why do you call me Kitten?"

"Because you're like a soft little kitten, all warm and cuddly; don't ever lose that."

Smiling she replied, "Can we start with a shower together?"

"That's a good beginning." Aiee-ya– we're not only tasting the fruit; we're feasting on it!

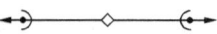

The lessons continued for another three days, which included an overnight in Kanapoli at the Sheraton. Clarice wished class could have gone on forever.

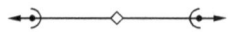

Returning home there were six messages on the answering machine from Allison; once from Beijing, twice from Shanghai, and three times from Hong Kong. She was worried sick that there had been an accident. Tommy reached her at the Ambassador Hotel in Kowloon.

"Where have you been, is Clarice all right?" she worriedly demanded from half-way around the world.

"She's fine; I took her with me to Honolulu. It took longer than I thought to sign up the investment group – they work on a different time-table over there. I'm sorry I worried you."

"Yes, well next time you call my office if something unforeseen comes up; they'll always know where I am."

"Yes dear – my fault."

"Everything is going as planned here. I should return on schedule; is Clarice okay?

"She's fine; don't worry so much."

"It's what Mothers do. Goodbye, this call is costing a fortune."

"Yes dear; goodbye."

Clarice was true to her word; at home she was the perfect daughter, well behaved, a good student. Allison was proud of her; she wasn't rebellious like many of her friends' children. Clarice was exceptional, she excelled at ballet; growing more beautiful every day. As her father, Tommy was also proud of his daughter; no parent had a better offspring. His mind easily switched from lover to father; there was no confusion.

Whenever Allison left on a trip Tommy and Clarice would seamlessly change back to lovers. They would drive to another city where Tommy booked them into adjoining rooms. There'd be tours, laughing, dinners, and all-night love. Tommy knew it couldn't last, but as someone once said, 'In for a penny; in for a pound.'

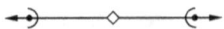

Midway through her nineteenth year Clarice missed a period and began for no reason to occasionally vomit in the morning. Allison was worried she had caught the stomach flu and took her to see a doctor. The test results came back that Clarice was pregnant.

Allison exploded, "What have you done? Who is the father? Is it that boy in your ballet class?"

Clarice remained silent; she was not about to disclose who the father was regardless of her Mother's threats.

Tommy couldn't believe it, they'd always taken precautions. Could she be having an affair with someone else? *What a mess,* he thought. *This is terrible; if I'm the father, the child might come out a savant or idiot. How could this have happened?*

Clarice received a lot of verbal abuse from both parents but she remained silent; not divulging anything regarding who the father might be. It was only at night in her room with the lights off that she smiled and hoped the baby would be all right; it would be her secret, her gift from God and the man she loved so desperately.

"Tommy, we've got to do something; she won't tell us who the father is – she won't consent to an abortion. What are we going to do?"

"I don't know dear; we could send her to Hong Kong and have the child adopted. May I have some more tea?"

They were sitting in the breakfast nook, finishing their morning repast. Clarice was off to school as she had not yet begun to show. "She's strong willed; she'd see through our idea and maybe run away."

Both stared out into the garden wondering how the Gods above could do this to them. Allison was the next to speak, "I have an idea. Doesn't your insurance broker, Leland Wong, have a boy that just graduated from college? Maybe we could make a match that would save our faces?"

Leland insured all Tommy's properties; it could be a good move financially that would strengthen and consolidate future business. "You mean Leland's son, Nelson? He's working for his Father. I don't know – how would we approach it?"

"I'll talk to Betty Wong; it would be good for both our families. We've got to move fast before Clarice starts to blossom out."

"It does seem like a good idea, what about Clarice – shouldn't we talk to her?"

"Clarice? She's our daughter; she'll do what we tell her. You explain to her this is her best option unless she wants an abortion, or go to Hong Kong. You're her father – you tell her what we're going to do and she'd better follow orders – or else!"

They both sat in silence finishing their tea. Finally, Tommy slid back his chair and stood up, "You're right dear, it is the best we can do. I'll have a talk with Clarice when she gets home from school. Now, I've got to get down to the office, we're breaking ground on that Fremont property and I want to be there."

"Honey, it's your only option; you don't want an abortion and I know you don't want to give the child up for adoption…"

"But Dad I don't even know Nelson; I've only met him a few times at your Christmas parties."

"He's a good kid – a college graduate – he works for his father learning the insurance business. He'll be able to take care of you and the baby."

"I still don't like the idea…"

"Young lady you'll do what we say. It is a tradition that cannot be broken"

"That's so old fashioned…"

"Old fashioned, or not, it is what respectable Chinese families do; it worked for your mother and I, it will work for you. Now get used to the idea. Your Mother is arranging a dinner with the Wongs, you and Nelson will have the chance to get acquainted and maybe he'll ask you out."

"Oh, Dad…"

"Don't 'Oh Dad' me. By the way, who is the father?"

"Who do you think; there's only one man in my life. Only one man I will ever love."

Tommy stared at her dumb-founded at the realization he was the father. "God; I hope the child comes out normal."

During the semi-formal dinner Clarice noted that Leland Wong was not at all like her Dad; fat and bald with hair growing out of his nose and ears; he was all business with no sense of humor. His wife, Betty, acquiesced to Leland on all subjects with replies of, "Yes dear," "That's right, dear," and "I agree, dear."

Nelson was tall and skinny; he had a big Adam's apple and nose. He quietly stared at Clarice throughout the meal making her uncomfortable. After dinner Clarice, under orders from her mother, nervously invited him to look at the roses in their back garden.

"We have a gardener that takes care of them, Mom loves them; they smell good. Try this one."

Nelson bent over smelling the large rose in full bloom. Turning he stuttered, "Y – you – ar – are sure a lot prettier than I thought. – Y - you're beautiful."

"I think I have my Mother's genes, she's beautiful too."

"N - not like you," he continued… "Wa - what do you think of our parents d - doing this?"

"I think it is an old custom…there's nothing I can do about it."

Becoming bolder, his stammer diminished, "I - agree, however it – it will strengthen our families and one day you and I will become very ri – rich…"

"I don't care about money; I care about life."

"Y – You don't care about money because you've always had plenty. I – I will provide well for us and we will learn to love each other; it is the way of our culture."

"Come on, let's go back in; our parents will wonder what happened to us." As she turned and started up the path to the house Nelson reached out and took her hand; his was wet and clammy, she wanted to cry.

The wedding was a gala affair with a reception for one hundred fifty at the grand ballroom of the Silver Dragon in Oakland. All the major players in Chinatown were invited as were the most important City officials and politicians. Tommy and Allison pulled out the stops to impress with a grand show of pomp.

Nelson and Clarice flew off for a week in Bali courtesy of her father. Nelson said he couldn't be gone any longer because his Dad needed him to set up the new computers in the office.

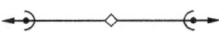

Tamar-Christine (TC) arrived with a loud yell; a healthy, smiling, six weeks premature baby with a full head of hair, a button nose and her Mother's beautiful eyes. Clarice had watched her own weight and together with her ballet exercises made what was in fact a full-term birth effortlessly easy. Clarice adored her. Nelson was mystified by all the goings-on and stayed longer hours at the office. Allison couldn't help but love her first grandchild. Tommy breathed a big sigh of relief that the child appeared healthy and normal in all respects. *Things are going to work out all right,* he thought. *She is normal, funny, and beautiful like her mother; not at all what I expected.*

TC was only five months old when Clarice announced she was pregnant again; this time it was Andrew, and he bore a strong resemblance to Nelson. He was quieter than TC who took an immediate liking to her younger brother.

Thirteen months later Benjamin came along; Clarice was beginning to think she was nothing more than a baby machine, popping out children on an assembly line. She loved the children, but was exhausted from constantly being a mother to all of them. Thank God Nelson was his employer's son. When she demanded a bigger house and a part-time caretaker it was provided by the grandfathers without question.

Tommy was friendly with a builder in Danville, an up-scale town over the hills from Piedmont. The suburb community had good schools, no crime, and was filled with quiet, upper middle-class status seeking young professionals. They purchased a four-bedroom, three-bath, two-story hillside home for $100,000 under market thanks to Tommy's connection.

After a hectic move, life settled down once more to normal. Nelson's father chipped in to pay the salary for Ani, a Slovakian girl recommended by the Agency. Clarice became especially fond of her, learning to trust her good judgment. Seven years older than Clarice, Ani was slim, trim, and tall. She wore her long blond hair in braids, and possessed a warm friendly smile. Ani took command. The children liked and obeyed her; she did the laundry, the shopping, and often prepared the meals. The two of them formed a comfortable, friendly relationship sharing the household workload and occasionally a weekend game of tennis when Nelson was home. She was a Godsend.

Tommy dropped by one day to take Clarice to lunch. It had been weeks since they'd shared any time together. "So, how's life treating you?"

"Oh Dad, thank you so much for helping with the house; each of the children have their own room. Nelson has a private study and I have Ani to help. Life has indeed gotten easier," she said as she dug into her Caesar salad laced with fried chicken.

"How are the children? I'm sorry your Mother and I have been so busy; we never seem to have enough time." Tommy admired Clarice's figure; after three children she still was a very attractive girl.

"The kids are doing fine; TC is my little helper with Anthony and Benjamin. She loves her brothers."

"And, how is Nelson; Leland says he is a workaholic."

"I know; that's all Nelson thinks about is business and making money. At home he's what I call a Three-Minute-Man," she replied with an edge to her voice.

Tommy had never heard that expression before, "What do you mean by that?"

"I mean once a week, on Saturday night, we perform sex for three minutes before he rolls over and goes to sleep. Except for the vibrator you gave me, I haven't had an orgasm in years!" she exclaimed in low tones.

"What, I don't believe it – not you," he said smiling.

Stabbing a chicken strip, she continued, "He's absolutely the worst in bed. I've tried teaching him some of the things you showed me and he says he doesn't like doing it that way. His idea of foreplay is to tell me I'm beautiful. He thinks making love is for making babies."

Tommy was surprised at his daughter's outburst. While it was true, they had not had sex since she became pregnant with TC, he assumed Nelson as a young man was satisfying her. Looking at her angrily expressing her frustration he marveled; *she is still killer-attractive and I am still stark-staring-mad.*

Changing the subject Clarice asked, "And how is Mom?"

"Your Mother is doing very well she sends her love. Her business is booming, she's opened another office in Chinatown, San Francisco, and spends much of her time conducting tours to China. I moved into your old room because I snore and disturb her sleep. She's always tired or busy thinking about her business."

"Why is Mom like that I wonder?"

"I think it is because she can't separate things; she can't put things away; everything is always on her mind. You and I have always been able to compartmentalize our life so the left hand doesn't interfere with the right."

"I guess. Do you want dessert?"

"No, let's go."

Taking Clarice home they were driving by a Holiday Inn when Tommy smiling nodded towards the sign and suggested, "How about one for old time's sake, Kitten?"

Looking up at the hotel sign and looking at her father smiling at her, Clarice replied with a mischievous grin, "Why not; one for the road. But we've got to make it a quickie Daddy."

"Anything for my little kitten."

It was good – very good – both felt exhausted and drained. The shower, the sex, was like old times.

Nine months later little Charlene exploded into the world with a set of lungs bigger than TC.

PART TWO

Two's Company

Allison was just heading out the door when the phone rang. Picking it up a voice on the other end said, "Good morning I'm Mike with Holiday Inn."

Thinking it was a sales call she was about to hang up when the voice continued, "Is Mister Chan available?"

"No, he's already left for the office. Who is this again?"

"I'm Mike the front desk clerk at the Dublin Holiday Inn. Please tell Mister Chan we have his jacket on a hanger behind the front desk; he left it in his room."

"Are you sure you have the right phone number?"

"That's the number sewn into his jacket; is this Clarice Chan?"

"No this is his wife, Allison."

"Oh, I think I have the wrong number." With a click Mike hung up.

Confused and mystified Allison sat for a moment before calling her office to say she'd be an hour late and to hold all her calls. She then drove over to Dublin where a gas station attendant directed her to the Holiday Inn down the block.

Walking through the double glass doors and up to the front desk she announced to the girl behind the counter, "I'm Mrs. Chan, I understand you have my husband's jacket."

The clerk turned around and looked through a few articles hung up on a rack. Selecting a white coat, she turned back to Allison, "Is this it?"

Allison immediately recognized the Ralph Lauren Polo jacket she had given him for his birthday a few years back.

"Yes, that's it. His name, Tommy Chan, and phone are sewn on the inside pocket – see it?"

The girl looked inside the garment, "Yes, I see it; a nice jacket she added as she handed over the coat.

Reaching for the piece Allison asked, "Is Mike on duty?"

"I think he's on his break; he's probably having coffee in the kitchen. Is there something I can do?"

"No, I would like to speak with Mike; how long before he comes back?"

"He just left; I think it will be at least fifteen minutes."

Allison checked her watch before replying, "Never mind, I have the jacket. Oh, does Mister Chan come here often?"

"I'm sorry, I can't answer that; the company doesn't allow us to give out any information about our guests."

"Thank you."

"No problem."

Driving back to her Oakland office Allison noted Dublin was adjacent to Danville. Mike had called her Clarice. The two of them had taken trips together when she was out of town. TC looks different than her brothers; she resembles Tommy in her nose and extroverted personality. *Could Clarice and Tommy…? That's ridiculous… Still…* By the time she got to her office she needed two cups of tea to settle her nerves. She was going to have a word with Tommy tonight.

Presenting Tommy with his Polo jacket as he walked in the door she blurted, "Mike at Holiday Inn called and said you'd left this in your room."

Tommy looked at her and reached out for the jacket, "Thanks."

"Thanks? What were you doing in a hotel in Dublin?"

"It was when you were gone; I had dinner with Clarice and Nelson. It was late; I had a few drinks, so I checked into the hotel…"

"Liar!" She exploded, "Mike called me Clarice; the two of you were in that room! How could you?"

"How could I what?"

"How could you bed your own daughter?"

"Allison that's nonsense; I don't know what you're talking about…"

"You know – we've been married twenty-four years – I know when you're lying!" she was so angry tears were streaming down her face. "God damn you; I should have guessed…"

"Allison there's nothing to guess; you're imagining all this. Clarice and I are father and daughter…"

"Liar – Liar – I can see it in your face; you are lying. Call her – call Clarice. I want her over here; I want to talk to her. It's time we all had a talk. Get her on the phone!"

Tommy was stunned by Allison's outburst. *What a dumb thing I did leaving that damned jacket hanging in the closet. Damn!* "I'll call Clarice, but its dinner time I don't think she'll be able to come over until tomorrow."

"You tell her I want to talk to her. You tell her to come over as soon as she gets Nelson off to work. Tell her this is serious. Tell her– Oh, damn!" Reaching for a Kleenex, she blew a mighty blast. "Damn it all to Hell," she cried into the tissue as she wiped her nose.

Tommy had never heard her swear before.

Picking up the phone he dialed Clarice's number; after three rings, she answered, "Hi Dad, I'm really busy – I'm serving dinner; can you call back?"

"Kitten, this will only take a minute. Your Mother is very upset. She wants you to come over tomorrow morning. I know it sound ridiculous but she thinks we've been sleeping together; she's very upset."

"What? Dad, what are you talking about? Oh damn, my meat is burning – I'll call you back," and she hung up.

The meat didn't burn. Clarice fed Andrew, Benjamin, and little Charlene before tucking them in bed. Nelson, TC, and Clarice ate a simple meal of spaghetti & meatballs with a tossed salad. TC brushed her teeth; Clarice tucked her in bed giving her hugs and kisses. The boys were asleep in their bunk beds. Charlene wanted a story read from the book her grandmother had given her. Nelson had already dozed off by the time she crawled under the covers.

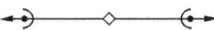

"Where is she? It's after eleven; she should have been here an hour ago. Try her phone again," Allison was working up a full head of steam."

"Dear, I've tried three times already, there's no answer. I hope she's not in an accident."

"Call Nelson, find out if she was all right when he left for work."

"I can't do that; what will he think. Let's keep this all between ourselves."

"We'll drive over; I want to talk to that young lady."

They drove to Danville in silence. Ani answered the door, saying she thought Clarice had left early to go shopping. TC was in preschool; the two boys were playing on the rug with their little sister; everything appeared normal. They drove home in silence. Both left for their respective offices.

That evening just after seven Nelson called to say Clarice had left him.

Tommy answered the phone, "What are you talking about, Nelson?"

"When I got home Mister Chan there was a note tucked into my cufflink box. It was from Clarice; all it said was; I'm leaving you – Look after the children. I don't understand."

"I don't either. Is her car there?"

"No sir, it's gone."

"Is Ani there?"

"No sir, she was waiting for me when I got home. She fed the children and left before I found the note. I don't know what to think. TC wants to know where her Mommy is – what am I going to do?"

"Take it easy – she's probably been disturbed by something. Were you two fighting? I'm sure she'll be home before long."

"No, we never fight; should I phone the police?"

"No. No, don't do that; it will just cause more problems. I'll talk with her mother; she may have some ideas."

However, Allison didn't have any ideas and Clarice didn't come home. Ani gave a short notice, quitting at the end of the week. The children cried and fought with the replacement sent out by the Agency.

It was two weeks before Clarice's car was found abandoned on a side road in the Delta. It was sitting on its axles; the wheels, hubcaps, and tires stolen. Vandals had stripped it, stolen the license plate, and broken the windows. It was identified by the VIN number. When the police notified Nelson of the find, the officer requested a Missing Persons Report. They interviewed him before deciding it was either a suicide or missing person; either way, they had more important business to attend. A runaway Chinese wife was not high on their agenda regardless of how well-off the family.

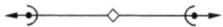

Lying on the couch she'd finished her third book in five days when Ani walked in the door, "You look cozy on the couch, what did you do today?"

"Read and slept; this is the first time I've had any time to myself in ages," Clarice replied as she put the book down and stretched. "I can't thank you enough for letting me use your couch; I am still absolutely-totally-bummed out. I miss the children, particularly TC, terribly. However, I know this is the right choice; better for me, better for them."

"It's okay; I knew you were in big trouble or you'd never have asked for my help. I picked up my check from the Agency; there's enough to drive back to New York and my Cousin Lily's place. Do you want to come along and share the driving?"

Clarice had emptied her secret hiding place of the $9,252. she'd managed to skim off the household budget over the last five years, "I can help with the few bucks I have and the driving. Sure, I'd love to tag along."

They left the next morning in Ani's six-year-old Corolla sedan bound for Reno on Highway 80. Starting up the mountains east of Sacramento the scenery filled with scented pines trees, streams and little lakes. Clarice loved looking out the window; enjoying her new freedom. It was the first time she'd ever been on her own with not a soul telling her what she should be doing. On the drive neither spoke of anything personal. It was as though they had invoked a traveler's good manners to keep the conversation light and general. Ani was easy to be with – a good companion.

They spent the first night in a single room with twin beds in Sparks, Nevada. Splitting a roll of quarters, each gambled, and lost five dollars on the slot machines. Thus confirming what they had earlier discussed; that there must be more losers than winners. Otherwise, who paid for all those beautiful casinos?

Leaving early the next morning they adopted a schedule of two-hours-on and two-hours-off, changing places at rest stops along the way. Salt Lake City was ten hours down the road. Nevada and Utah, though mostly desert, were still beautiful in the early light. It was lucky the Corolla's air-conditioning worked, as after lunch at an Elko truck stop, it got really hot.

Watching Ani drive Clarice admired her confidence and comfortable take-charge attitude. "Ani, what is Slovakia like where you grew up?"

"I was born in a little village near Prague. The land is a lot like parts of California, except we have snow in the winter. Lots of farms and low, rolling hills; it was a good place."

"Does Ani stand for anything?"

"In Slovakia it means, 'very beautiful,' mother said I was a beautiful baby."

"You still are."

"Thank you, I just think I'm a normal Slovakian girl."

"Do you have any brothers or sisters?"

"Two sisters, I'm the youngest, and one older brother who was killed while serving in the Russian army. My Dad died eight years after world war two from injuries he received fighting the Germans."

"Gee, that was awful; did your mother remarry?"

"With three girls? – No chance of that. We moved to Prague where Mom got a job as a maid in one of the hotels. When they were old enough, my sisters joined her as maids."

"Why didn't they marry?

"Men are in short supply in Slovakia; wars have killed them off. There was no money for a proper dowry so they remained single."

"How did you get to America?"

"I made it a point to learn to speak good English in school: I didn't want to wind up a maid. I answered a newspaper classified advertisement for an au-pair placed by a married couple who had two kids in New York. The interview was easy; the man liked my body, the woman liked it that she could confide in me." That bought me a ticket to America and freedom.

"Why did you leave?"

"I lasted fifteen months. The man kept pinching my butt until I had black and blue marks all over it. The woman was a heavy drinker and a bitch when she was drunk, which was much of the time. I did like the children – they're going to have a rough time growing up. What about you? Were you born in America?"

"No, I was born in Hong Kong, it's a British colony next to China. We left there when I was seven years old. The Communists were threatening to invade the colony. My grandfather was afraid we'd be trapped if they took over. He had too many businesses to leave, but he told my Dad to get out before something bad happened."

"Do you have any brothers or sisters?"

"No, just me; mother was too busy to raise a family and dad was always making a deal."

"Don't you have any friends – anybody you're close with?"

"No, Mother always thought we were better than everybody; including all the kids I went to school with. She said their parents were nothing but tradesmen."

"It sounds like she is a snob."

"She is; she doesn't like the lower classes. I think she wanted me to be a virgin bride for a rich Tai-pan:"

"What is a Tai-pan?"

"It is a man who is a supreme boss – a rich leader with lots of money and power."

"Nelson doesn't seem like a tai-pan."

"I got pregnant."

"Oh, is Nelson the father?"

"He thinks he is."

"Oh."

Both rode along in silence for a few miles until Clarice continued, "Dad's different, he likes to joke with everybody."

"You like your Dad?"

"A lot."

The little Corolla hummed along at 70 mph on cruise control as the two drifted off into their own thoughts.

"I'm beat, how about you?" Ani asked.

"Me too, America sure is huge when you drive it."

"We've only covered seven hundred miles; we've got another twenty-three hundred to go."

"Wow, how long do think it will take us?"

"If we do four hundred miles a day, we should be at Lily's in six more days."

"Except for Hawaii this is the furthest I've been away from home in my life."

"I flew out to San Francisco. This is the longest road trip I've ever taken. Come on, let's get a sandwich at Arby's, hit the shower, and turn in."

"Okay."

Again, it was a single room with twin beds; Clarice had not confided in Ani about how much money she really had. Besides, it made sense sharing a room not just for cost, but security.

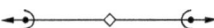

The motel in Cheyenne only had a room with a king-size bed.

"If it's okay with you, it's okay with me," Ani smiled.

"I'm alright with it, but let's get a pizza to-go and eat in the room; I'm tired," Clarice answered.

There was a liquor store next to the pizza joint and Ani suggested they get a bottle of Zinfandel to go with the pie.

"That sounds like another good idea; driving really tires me out."

The wine made the pizza taste better; upon reaching the last bite, they had finished the bottle. Both had a slight buzz from the delicious, 14% alcohol.

With a smile and a laugh Ani suggested they shower together to save water and time. Clarice agreed, feeling relaxed and slightly tipsy. Ani had a beautiful firm body; she'd shaved her pubic hair; her breasts were small and firm. Her long blond hair reached to the small over her back. The shower was a little small for the two of them, forcing them to make unintended body contact as they lathered.

"Will you soap and wash my back?" Ani asked. "I'll do yours if you'll do mine," she added.

"Sure, turn around." Clarice was careful to only wash down her back, leaving the cheeks and crack of Ani's butt alone. The warm water felt especially good splashing over both of them after the long drive.

"Thanks, now it's your turn," Ani said, "Hand me the soap."

Clarice passed the soap and wash cloth to Ani who started at the top and worked slowly down her back. She soaped and expertly massaged her butt; it felt good to Clarice as she relaxed letting Ani knead her tired muscles.

"Like it?" Ani asked.

"Love it," Clarice answered.

Ani gently washed the crack of her butt with a soapy hand, making sure there were plenty of suds for her sphincter. That felt good too, Clarice was becoming excited.

"Want me to do the front?" Ani asked.

"Not right now, I can do it myself," Clarice replied as she took back the soap and cloth.

"Come on, let's get out; I want to dive into that big, beautiful bed," Ani smiled warmly.

Clarice felt the excitement; something new was going to happen. Ani did have a gorgeous body and a wonderful touch.

It wasn't long before Ani had brought Clarice to the most explosive orgasm she'd had since first doing it with her father.

"Oh, God, don't stop – don't stop – I love it. Yes, there, right there – do it – Oh – oh – oh God." Ani was good, a little like her father, yet in some ways better. Clarice didn't need to worry about getting pregnant and Ani truly showed amazing talent.

"I love the way you kiss me down there. Do it with your finger…"

"In your butt?"

"Be gentle."

They spent another two days in Cheyenne swimming in the pool, relaxing in the Sun, eating leisurely meals accompanied by that lovely red Zinfandel. There were lots of hot showers and making love on the big king-size bed. Clarice hadn't enjoyed sex so much in years. Ani was a wonderful lover, knowledgeable, patient, warm, and soft; she enjoyed bringing Clarice to climax.

It wasn't until Lincoln, Nebraska that Ani suggested Clarice try her electric razor. "Your pubes tickle my nose – do you mind?"

"No, I've been thinking about it; I like the way yours look, but I'm afraid after four kids my pussy is a bit wrinkled."

"It's not that bad. I'll shave you the first time. Be prepared the buzz of the electric razor may turn you on. You'll feel better if you don't wear any panties afterwards; let the breeze caress and cool your fun-factory. Believe me, you'll love it."

"I won't mind; if it does turn me on you can finish the job, okay? I wear panties out of habit I guess. If you don't – I don't – okay?"

"Okay; I'm glad we found each other."

"Me too."

"When you're ready sometime; how about you returning the favors…"

"Oh Ani, I'm ready – I'm ready. I hope I can do you as good as you do me."

"You will, sweet-love – you will; I'm a good teacher."

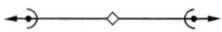

Driving down the highway the conversation became more spontaneous and easier. "The first time? I was twelve, my cousin was eighteen; she was very pretty and always liked to joke. We were spending the weekend at my aunt and uncle's house. The adults had one bedroom; my sisters slept in sleeping bags in the living room; I bunked in with my cousin. Sometime during the night, I awoke when she was fondling my crotch and sucking on one of my nipples. She told me to be quiet and pulled off my panties before going down on me."

"WOW! What did you do?"

"Nothing; I liked it. My cousin was an expert, making me feel really fantastic and it was exciting having a secret that nobody knew about."

"I don't know what I'd have done. It sounds so weird; did you ever do it with boys"

"I grew up thinking; girls played with girls, boys with boys, and girls and boys only had sex to make babies. It wasn't until I was a teenager, I learned girls and boys did it for fun too."

"What about now; do you do it with men too?"

"I like a man who is a gentle man, clean, and smells good; one who is not afraid to experiment. I don't like crude low-life's of either sex."

"What happened to your cousin?"

"She married a man and had three children; she's big and fat now."

"You certainly started out early."

"What about you? Who got you pregnant?"

"A man I was in love with – a gentle man – I'll tell you later; I don't want to talk about it right now."

It took them three weeks to drive to New York; they never slept in twin beds again. It was the best three weeks Clarice had ever spent in her life.

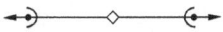

Lily lived in a townhouse on Long Island an hour's drive from Manhattan, where she owned an escort service. Never married, Lily was a big, warm, attractive, blond-haired woman in her mid-forties. It was a Sunday when she answered the doorbell chimes; her blue eyes lit up when she opened the front door and saw the two of them standing there. "Ani! Ani what a surprise," she exclaimed as she reached out to give her a big hug and kisses on both cheeks.

Smiling, Ani turned to Clarice, "Cousin Lily, I want you to meet my friend, Clarice."

Lily reached over giving Clarice a hug and kisses, "A friend of Ani's is a friend of mine," she said holding Clarice's hand.

"Come in, come in. Why didn't you tell me you were coming?"

"It was a long drive and I didn't know when we'd get here…"

"What happened to Natalie, the partner you went to California with?"

"A long story – we broke up. I took care of Clarice's children. I'll explain all it later."

"You both look tired; I'll get you some lunch. You must stay; the spare bedroom is all made up."

They carried their bags up the stairs to a lovely bedroom on the second floor adjacent to Lily's. The room was light and airy with paintings of pastoral landscapes hanging on the wall. A queen-size four poster canopied bed with lots of pillows and a floral bedspread dominated the room. White lace curtains framed the window that opened to a view of Long Island bay.

"I hope you two won't mind sharing the bed," Lily shouted up from the kitchen.

Both looked at each other and smiled. "We won't mind Cousin Lily – it's perfect," Ani shouted back.

Over a two-hour lunch Ani brought Cousin Lily up to date; making it a point to leave out the very private details. Clarice shyly added a few comments. Lily guessed they were more than likely gay lovers. Nevertheless, that was none of her business.

"Well you two – you're here. How would you like to go to work for me? I have an escort service in Manhattan that could use two beauties like you."

"What does an escort do?" Clarice asked.

"You get paid to have dinner with the client. Sometimes you go to a play, or a party, you pay the client compliments. You are window dressing and enjoyable company."

"Do we have to go to bed with them?"

"Not as an escort. I charge three hundred dollars and you keep two of the three; which is more than what I do for the other girls I have working for me. I can book you three dates a week."

Clarice gave a questioning look to Ani who turned to Lily saying, "We'll give it a try. Can we stay with you until we get some money coming in?"

"Of course, but you'll want to move down to Greenwich Village to be closer to your work. This is a long commute. I'll advance you some money for clothes and if you don't mind; I'd like to change your names."

"Our names – what's wrong with our names?"

"Nothing's wrong with your names, it's just the clients want a sense of adventure – of mystery. Talking with you both I've come up with Sofia and Jade; what do you think?

Ani grasped the idea right away; it took Clarice a few moments to realize the advantage of using a fictitious name. Nobody would know her; it would be a new beginning. The more she thought of it, the better she liked it.

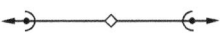

Monday, they rode into Manhattan in Lily's new Lexus. Clarice was in awe of all the people and traffic. The office was smartly decorated, looking a little like a theatrical casting agency. Lily introduced the girls to her secretary, Madeline, "Sofia is my cousin and Jade is her friend, they're coming to work for us."

"You'll like working for Lily, she's fabulous," the smartly dressed older woman said as she gave them the once over; noting their somewhat common clothes.

"Madeline, call up the woman you know at Nordstrom's and tell her two of my girls are coming over and they need outfitting."

"Yes Lily."

"And tell her to try to keep it under a thousand dollars each."

"Yes Lily.

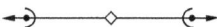

Sofia and Jade were booked three, sometimes four, nights a week. Lily took another hundred out of their pay until they had paid her back for the clothes she'd bought them. They moved into a cramped studio apartment in Greenwich Village. Ani sold her car as it was a liability in New York.

Initially the job was exciting, but the steady grind of dinners and boring customers with only a day's rest between jobs took their toll.

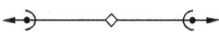

"It must be interesting being the District Manager for Acme Ball Bearings, does it pay well?"

"You mean you're in charge of all the hiring west of the Mississippi? Fascinating! I'd love dessert, thank you."

"What does a comptroller do?"

Whenever possible, Lily booked them on double dates, which made the evenings more fun. 'Sofia' was a direct descendant from Romanian royalty and 'Jade' a great-great-grand-daughter of the last Emperor of China. Together, they'd play-act off each other.

One-night Lily had booked the two of them with Mister Bradley, a portly man of about sixty, who wanted the company of both of them for dinner. He was a gentleman who laughed at their play-acting; making them more spontaneous. As they were finishing dessert his voice changed as he turned serious, "How would you ladies like to make some real money?"

They'd both heard this line before, "You mean go to bed with you?" Ani returned.

"No, I mean you both going to bed with each other – and let me watch?"

"What?" Jade incredulously replied.

"I mean five thousand dollars to let me watch."

There was a pause as Sofia caught the sly nod from Jade before answering, "I think you bought yourself a show."

Mr. Bradley had a suite at the Ritz Carlton. True to his word, he unlocked a leather briefcase by the nightstand and extracted a neatly bank-banded stack of one hundred-dollar bills. "There's fifty there; do you want to count them?"

Sofia reached for the cash fanning the stack to break up their crisp stiffness "No, Jade and I believe you to be a man of your word; do you have an envelope?

Mr. Bradley located one from the hotel stationary folder and handed it to her.

Sofia tucked the bulging packet into her purse before turning around to boisterously announce, "Show time!"

She played the aggressor, Jade the shy, hesitant, novice.

Sofia lifted Jade's chin with her hand, gently brushing her lips with a moist tongue.

"I've never done this before," Jade shyly whispered, "You won't hurt me?"

"I'll be gentle, you'll love it – I promise," Sofia replied as she reached around to unzip Jade's dress. The garment fell to the floor revealing Jade without a bra, wearing only a thong bikini. Sofia kissed Jade's nipples, slowly working her way down to her navel as she helped Jade out of her thong. Both were clean shaven.

Mr. Bradley, who had changed into a terrycloth robe, was sitting in an armchair slowly stroking himself while watching the two perform. His breath coming in short gasps and snorts.

Glancing over at Mr. Bradley, they enjoyed turning him on. He had mentioned earlier he promised his wife he would not go to bed with any prostitutes while in New York, but with a wink added, "She didn't say I couldn't eyeball."

Ani and Clarice fell naturally into the act like they'd rehearsed it; discovering a talent they didn't know the other possessed. Both were both born actresses; each ping-ponging off the other's action.

The climax was just that; Clarice moaning and faking an orgasm from Ani going down on her; Ani shouting and oohing as she rubbed her clit on Clarice's leg. Both timed it perfectly as Mr. Bradley shot semen all over the hotel's robe - a grand finale.

When Ani told Lily about how they put on a performance with Clarice playing the shy partner she was enthralled, "That was creative genius; you two are going to make a lot of money."

Dutifully they presented the envelope to Lily, who counted out forty of the newly printed one hundred-dollar notes. "You earned it; twenty percent is enough for the house. I think you've graduated to bigger game." Lily then went on to explain how she also ran a little side endeavor that made her a lot of money but was a bit illegal.

"Lily, we couldn't do that three times a night, we'd be exhausted."

"Who said anything about three times a night? I'm thinking of the top one percent of the one percent, they've got the money and love a good time. I've got a lot of connections. Five thousand is just the start; you're gonna be rich – really rich."

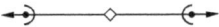

During their second gig the customer asked if they could dress like nurses; he wanted to put on a show for some visiting doctors. This led to airline stewardesses, nuns, teacher/school girl, and a whole closet full of costumes. Sofia was usually the aggressor, Jade the innocent, shy, femme. Occasionally their roles reversed; Jade as the Dragon Lady, and Sofia the bashful missionary, or slave-maid, were examples. Both played their parts to the hilt; enjoying the roles while entertaining the clientele. Clarice particularly like it when Ani played the part of a masseuse and she, the innocent customer. Ani gave a terrific massage; the orgasms were real.

It was only occasionally the act would include going to bed with the customer; that increased the price to ten thousand dollars. Lily was generous, keeping her commission to twenty-percent. Ani reminded Clarice; the John's were almost all Three-Minute-Men – it was just part of the business.

Life got good; they moved into an upscale apartment with a view. Jade had her breasts surgically firmed and her pussy trimmed to what the plastic surgeon called, the Barbie Doll look. She turned down his suggestion to increase her bust to a 36C; Jade wanted them to remain as a young girl. She did accept his other proposition of fifty percent off in exchange for a roll in the hay – another three-minute-man.

The procedures did make her appear years younger; forging greater confidence. Jade looked like a young teenager and accordingly the price went up. Through exercise Sofia stayed in athletic trim without an ounce of fat on her tall, lithe, golden brown body compliments of a tanning salon. They were a striking pair; the talk of the town.

Frederick Duponte Jr. (His friends called him Freddy.) was hosting a fortieth birthday bash for his long-time pal, Gerry Schwartz. Both came from wealthy families that provided them with generous allowances. Freddy wanted something special for his friend and guests. Therefore, it was logical that he contacted Lily for party favors.

"Lily I want those two broads you have to put on a show and I want at least a half dozen hookers for the guests."

"You mean Sofia and Jade; what sort of act do you want them to perform?"

"I don't care as long as it's over-the-top sexy. Oh, and I want the two available for Gerry and me."

"That will cost you a bundle…"

"Lily, you know I don't care, you're the best – I want to host a first-class orgy that my friends will remember. I'll give you the final count later; I'm thinking to use my apartment but I'm open to ideas."

"Your place is good as long as you don't invite an army. You know we're talking in the neighborhood of twenty thousand dollars."

"Not to worry; I'll give you a final count later this week. Oh, and no Bimbo's; I want only class hookers."

"I don't employ Bimbos, you know that."

Freddy's apartment took up a fourth of the fifteenth floor of one of the poshest buildings in Manhattan, measuring over fifty-five hundred square feet, five bedrooms, seven bathrooms. His father had bought it when the building was still in the planning stage.

FORBIDDEN FRUIT

At thirty-nine years old Freddy put on a grand show of being among the idle rich. He kept his five-foot eleven and one hundred-sixty-pound physique buff. His mother said he had the blond, wavy hair of Robert Redford and the blue bedroom eyes of Paul Newman. A twinkling, mischievous, grin, together with the dimples in his cheeks never failed to bring the opposite sex to boil. In fact, he was the idle rich; the money was his father's, and a mother who hands-down, adored their only son.

The father, Frederick Duponte, Sr. correctly guessing there would be a boom after the GIs came home from World War II, together with the government provided the GI Bill of Rights, he'd built over 10,000 track homes in the Los Angeles basin. There wasn't a farm or airport that he had not made an offer on. His current interest was building shopping centers; he owned twenty-two. In his early seventies, he was a power-house of a man. Commanding his empire from the twenty-five-story building he erected in Beverly Hills to house his vast holdings; one floor for each project. Strong men quivered in his presence; he was a big game hunter, an advisor to Presidents, he was afraid of no man or beast – except Mary-Belle, his wife.

At twenty-two, she was Miss Alabama before becoming runner up to Miss America forty years ago. Ten years her senior, Frederick fell instantly in love with this beautiful, captivating, strong willed girl with the lovely soft Southern accent. They made a perfect pair; Mary-Belle charmed the husbands while forging warm friendships with the wives. She produced one son, Freddy, whom she spoiled rotten from the womb onward.

Frederick had hoped his son would follow in his footsteps, but that was not to be. Freddy was expelled from the Swiss boarding school for setting fire to the sports scoreboard and propositioning his history teacher. Completing prep school in England; his grades were not good enough for Eton or Oxford. Frederick Senior endowed a wing at the University of Southern California (Also known as the University of Spoilt Children). Freddy attended one year before dropping out to crew with a classmate from England, on the colleague's father's yacht in Antigua.

Mary-Belle said Freddy just needed some time to make up his mind. Frederick decided he had a son who never was going to make up his mind, unless it was which party, or where to spend his summers.

Long ago Freddy had made up his mind; his God-given call was to spend as much of his parent's vast fortune as he could in order to keep the currency in circulation. After all he surmised, why should all that green sit molding in some bank vault? Besides, his mother loved hearing of his exploits and adventures with the ladies.

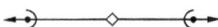

A young, good looking butler let them in, "Mr. Duponte will be along shortly. You can change into costume in there." He formally announced as he led them to Freddy's master suite.

"Have you ever seen any place like this?" Jade marveled as she gazed around the living room, "Look at that sculpture."

A tall, gold colored, nude replica of Michelangelo's David with a female's bust stared back at them. "It's well done, but it's weird. I hope this guy isn't into S&M." Sofia answered as she looked around the posh surroundings.

"Me too; Lily said he's kinky but not into anything that will hurt us."

They remained in the bedroom waiting for Freddy. The man-servant brought them hot tea. A half hour later Freddy showed up all smiles and lightness. "You two look better in person than you do performing. I caught one of your acts a few months ago at the police commissioner's retirement party. Where did you get the cop uniforms?"

"They rent everything." Sofia replied.

"It's Sofia, isn't it? What are you going to be tonight?"

"We could do a nun and school girl or how about a routine using the other girls as slaves?"

Freddy let out a laugh, "Do the slave gig; Gerry will love having a slave to order around; his wife wears the pants at home. Wait in here until Mario comes for you – excuse me, Mario is my major-domo, butler, cook, and general all-around gofer – I want to get the party going a bit. Oh, where are the working girls Lily said were coming over?"

Jade answered, "They should be here anytime. Do you want them to wait in here with us?"

"Yeah – you're Jade, aren't you – I want everything to be a complete surprise." Freddy gave Jade an admiring once-over, "You and Sofia are going to fuck Gerry and me you know?

"Yes, we know," Sofia responded matter-of-factly.

"Jade, you're with me, okay? Sofia, you've got Gerry. I'll have Mario set up some sodas for the girls. They'll be grass at the party and you can smoke as much as you want after you perform, okay?"

Six young women arrived fifteen minutes later looking like they belonged in college. "Sorry we're late; the damned limo didn't show up on time. Lily was furious," the brunette leader apologized to Sofia as they threw their bags on the bed. "This is some place, huh?"

"It sure is; did Freddy tell you we are going to wait here until he gives us the signal?" Sofia answered as she dug out some costumes from her bag.

"Yeah, it's like a Broadway production; the rich sure do live differently, huh?"

"They do, and they pay well so let's give them their money's worth." Sofia answered.

"I've got a million-dollar pussy and its itching for a payday." The leader smilingly shot back as everyone nervously laughed, thus breaking the unsaid tension.

A light knock on the door was the signal to go to work.

Sofia wrapped her long blond braided hair closely around her head. She was wearing a rolled-up sleeved white shirt with epaulets opened in the front to partially reveal her bra-less suntanned breasts. She had on riding breeches and boots and carried a short riding crop. Back erect, she was very-much the Aryan slave-master as she marched in, leading her chained slave girls. Heads down, eyes down, they were nude except for mini sarongs and a gold chain around their waists. Their breasts glistened from the light, perfumed, oil they'd applied.

The party had become silent at the change of pace brought on by Sofia's stern performance. Marching up to Freddy she announced, "You ordered slaves; these are the finest slave girls in America." Turning to Jade she continued as she lightly swatted her fanny, "I personally captured this one in Malaysia, she's a fine specimen, but doesn't speak much English. These came from a colleague in Arabia who deals in only the best white merchandise. They come from all over, Russia, Poland, Iceland, the Ukraine. He assured me they were all virgins, but I think he lied," she said with a straight face. "Mister Duponte, as the host, do you want to portion out the party favors?"

Freddy was pleased the merchandise was first class; he'd like to try them all himself, but manners dictated otherwise. Looking around the room he turned to an older man sitting in the Lounger, "Larry, how about this one?" He said, pointing to a girl with long blond hair covering her boobs.

"Looks good to me, what's her name, does she suck?" Larry shot back as the rest of the men nervously laughed.

"She is Nadia from the Ukraine and I'm told she can suck the chrome off a trailer hitch. Her brothers trained her well." Unsnapping the chain, Sofia flicked the girl's backside and ordered, "Go with that man – please him – make him happy or you'll taste the lash."

The girl timidly advanced towards Larry, dropping her sarong along the way revealing an exquisitely firm body with pointed nipples and a small sparkling diamond stone in her naval. She jumped up on his lap reaching down to fondle his crotch. "You like Nadia? You like to play?" she said in character.

"Do you have one that likes to do it doggy-style in the butt?" one of the guests yelled to Sofia.

"That would be Natasha; she prefers it to making babies." Sofia replied releasing the shyly smiling girl from bondage.

One by one they were all assigned a guest to satisfy until only Clarice remained. "Mr. Duponte, I will give you Jade, be gentle, she has never done it with a man."

"Thank you. What are you going to do?"

"I have had my eye on that one," she said pointing to Gerry. "He is the one I am going to make happy. Together, I will give him pleasure like he has never known." Further unbuttoning her shirt, she advanced towards Gerry who was wearing a big smile and a bulge in his pants. Reaching down to take his hand she continued, "Come to me, come; there is not an orifice I have that you cannot enter." They gently staggered off to the bedroom next to Freddy's.

Gerry wondered if he was going to be able to hold it until he got inside the beautiful, Teutonic blond goddess.

Freddy reached for Jade's hand while running his other hand down her butt. "Come on Jade, let's you and me go into the big bedroom."

"You like Jade?" she answered playing her roll.

"I like very much. You like?" he responded as he gently pinched her nipple.

"I make you feel good – I make you cum a lot." Jade replied following him demurely.

"And I make you feel good – I make you cum a lot, too"

The two giggled as Freddy closed and locked the door. He didn't want any disturbance; this was going to be good.

The two undressed and both were more than surprised by the other. Freddy had experienced a lot of hookers, but none quite like this. She was good, very good.

Clarice was surprised and pleased at Freddy's skill and control; he was definitely not a Three-Minute-Man. It had been a long time since Clarice had been so pleasured by a man. She came in his mouth. His prick was fantastic no matter which entrance he chose, she loved it. He was as good as Ani and he had that beautiful, wonderful, ever-hard, dick.

Freddy was just as amazed; Jade could do things with her mouth and hands that were as good as anything he'd ever had. Her pussy had muscles he didn't know existed and her ass was beyond belief.

Together they couldn't stop orgasming. *Thank God for Viagra*, he thought, *it was the best three hours I've known*. He finally stopped to say goodbye to his guests. The hookers all left; only Clarice and Ani remained.

"How'd it go with you and Gerry?" Freddy asked Sofia as he poured them a glass of chilled Sauvignon Blanc.

"A Two-Minute-Man," she replied.

Jade laughed as Freddy replied, "What do you mean by that?"

"Nothing it's an inside joke between Sofia and I."

"Never mind; how about we three dine up here? Jade has put me on the ropes."

"Sounds good, I'm hungry. Do you like escargot?" Sofia asked.

"Love them. Look it's getting late; you two jump in the shower, I'll order some catering and join you in a minute."

"Freddy, you sure have got stamina. Where do you get all your energy?"

"I'll never tell. Jade is out of this World and I think that all of us could have a lot of fun. Besides, three in a bed feels better."

A few lines of a song from the musical, Annie Get Your Gun, Anything you can do, I can do better, kept noodling around in his brain, only the words were, *Anything two can do, three can do better; three can do anything better than two.*

PART THREE

THREE'S A PARTY

A month later Lily called them into her office, "What did you two do to Freddy?"

"Nothing – why?" Jade worriedly replied.

"Well, whatever it was; keep doing it. He wants both of you to fly down to Miami for ten days on his yacht."

"Wow! How much is that going to cost him?" Sofia asked.

"I don't know the total expense, but you two are being hired out for fifteen thousand a piece."

"When do we leave? Has he sent over tickets?"

"I told him I wanted to check with you two first, if he was a nut case, I didn't want to risk your safety. You'll be flying in his own plane; I'll call him to let him know you agree."

"His own plane? His yacht? Who is this guy?"

"He's a throw-back to the Twenties; an idle rich gentleman whose parents are loaded. You two certainly impressed him; he couldn't say enough good things about both of you. Good luck."

Two days later a limo pulled up at the curb in front of Lily's building and drove them over to the executive section of La Guardia Airport where Freddy was waiting to usher them to the glistening white twin engine turboprop parked in front of the corporate terminal.

"You two look smashing! Thanks for agreeing to come."

Smilingly Sofia replied with a double entendre, "We'll come for you anytime, anyplace, and often Mr. Duponte."

"Today it's Captain Duponte. Let me show you the plane, the porters will handle your luggage." Freddy was wearing a white uniform shirt with gold four-bar epaulets – very-much the airline captain wannabe.

Walking through the lobby of the terminal Freddy was aware of the envious glances from the business men pausing in their conversations. *These two are special; they don't look or act like hookers. I hope they'll like my proposition.*

"The plane is a beauty; what kind is it?" Jade exclaimed.

"It's called a King Air; it can carry eight passengers plus a pilot and copilot. It's one of Dad's hand-me-downs; he gave it to me when he took delivery of his new Gulfstream. I like it because I can solo it; it doesn't take a crew like the Gulfstream"

"You have a pilot's license?" Jade marveled.

"Yes, but only a Private Pilot license, I'm not qualified to fly in the clouds so we'll go down to Miami low and fast. Besides, I like looking at the scenery."

The cabin was laid out with a three-seat divan on the left side that converted into a single bed. The right side contained a single high-backed plush reclining chair with a view of the cockpit. Behind that two seats of the same style faced each other with a collapsible table between them. When the table was stowed, the seats could be fully reclined to form a passable sleeping area. Aft of the seating area was a small galley big enough to hold a sink, fridge, and microwave. There was a separate toilet compartment with wash basin, followed by an inflight accessible baggage compartment.

Freddy offered Jade the copilot's seat, but she declined preferring to sit in the aft forward-facing recliner closest to the exit door. Sofia belted herself on the sofa opposite Jade. Both wanted to be next to the door in case something went wrong. However, Freddy was all business in the captain's seat; he wore earphones and talked to the controllers in a professional manner as they taxied out for takeoff.

The plane accelerated smoothly lifting off effortlessly. The women were impressed becoming aware of a side of Freddy they didn't realized existed.

Once the plane reached its cruise altitude Freddy engaged the autopilot and got out of his seat to join the girls in the back.

Alarmed, Sofia asked, "Who's flying the plane?"

"Relax, the plane is on autopilot coupled to a GPS which is programmed to take us to Miami. Anybody care for some coffee or tea?" he said as he poured himself a cup from a large thermos mounted to the bulkhead in the galley.

The girls preferred tea which Freddy made using teabags and hot water stored in the thermos next to the coffee. "How about a sandwich?"

Both declined, "It's too early to eat, the tea is just right, thank you Freddy," Sofia answered.

Taking a seat in the other recliner Freddy continued, "I have a special treat for both of you; I'm going to personally initiate you into a very exclusive club after we finish our drinks."

"Really? That sound exciting; what kind of a club is it?" Jade asked.

"The Three-Mile-High Club – very exclusive – as a matter of fact we will be the only members."

"What?" Sofia replied with a mischievous smile.

"The Three-Mile-High Club with three members; I like it." Freddy shot back. "We three, over three-miles high on this couch, not many can say they've done that. Let's get naked."

"Let's wait until we finish our drinks, I don't want to spill hot tea on my titties," Jade added with a laugh. "Freddy, you are crazy, you know."

"I know – don't you love it?"

"We do." Sofia said as she reached over to grab his crotch only to realize he already had an erection. *He is crazy; but a good crazy, I hope.*

The King Air hummed along on-course as the three of them fucked on the couch, in the chairs, and standing up against a bulkhead. All three couldn't get enough of each other; they balled, laughed, and snacked, the eleven-hundred-miles to the home of the Orange Bowl.

Freddy landed at Fort Lauderdale, not far from where he moored his yacht. They took a taxi to the Marina and walked down the dock to the end-tied fifty-foot Choey Lee motor yacht that was waiting patiently for her master.

"Is that yours? It's beautiful!" Jade exclaimed as her eyes traveled over the white, fiber glass hull and the varnished teak cabin with glistening stainless steel everywhere.

"It's another hand-me-down from Dad when he took delivery of his new eighty-footer. This is Mary-Belle – Dad named her after my Mom – she's a real lady. Like the plane, I prefer something I can operate myself without the need of a crew; they talk too much. She's a good, sturdy boat with two big Caterpillar diesel engines that give speed and range. Watch yourselves on the steps; don't trip upon boarding."

Both girls were nimble, happily hopping onboard through the open gate.

"Stow your stuff in the aft master stateroom while I check the engines and make sure she's ready for sea." Freddy's voice changed, becoming a captain again.

Jade thought it funny how one minute he could be a light-hearted playboy and the next, a no-nonsense captain. It did give her a secure feeling that Freddy took his duties seriously. The master stateroom had a huge king-sized bed with a large screen TV mounted for viewing while reclining on the bed.

Sofia opened one to the lockers looking for a place to hang their clothes. "Will you look at this?" she said to Jade. "Freddy sure likes sex toys."

Jade peered in at the various vibrators, dildos, and playthings, "It must be the captain in him; you'd have to be an engineer to operate all those things. I'm not convinced I'd like that dildo stuck in me; look at the size of it!"

"Look in this drawer, he's got a whole library of porn tapes; Freddy sure likes sex," Sofia announced.

"He certainly does, but he's rich and he's fun and he likes us, so let's enjoy the ride." Jade responded.

Mary-Belle came alive with a low throaty rumble from the big diesels. Freddy liked the sound of the engines – all that power at his fingertips when he moved the throttles gave him a rush. Jade and Sofia joined him on the bridge. A dockhand appeared and was standing by to cast off the lines.

Noting the wind and current Freddy leaned over the port side speaking to him in a voice just loud enough to be heard, "Castoff the stern line first, and I'll swing the stern out; then cast off the bow, okay?"

"Yes sir; ready when you are," came the reply.

"Jade you go aft to take the line; wave when you have it onboard, I don't want anything to foul the propellers."

"Yes sir, Captain," she said with a smile and salute.

"Sofia you go forward and pull the line on board when the dockhand casts it off and give me a high sign after you have it all on deck."

"Yes Captain," she said mock saluting.

They both took up their stations as Freddy motioned to the dockhand to cast off the stern line. Jade pulling hand-over-hand brought the line on board, shouting, "I got it," displaying the end of the line. Freddy put the right engine in Forward and the left in Reverse at idle power. The yacht slowly pivoted stern-first out into the channel. "Okay, cast off the bow," he commanded.

The dockhand coiled and threw the line up to Sofia who caught it, shouting, "bow lines on board, Captain."

Freddy switched the right engine to reverse as the yacht slowly back into the stream until the big boat had the room to maneuver forward.

Joining him on the bridge Sofia asked, "How come you backed out of the mooring?"

"Because a boat handles like a forklift, not a car; everything is accomplished from the rear, the engines and rudders are in the back. Seldom do I cast off the bow first. Get me a beer from the galley fridge will you Jade?"

"Yes sir…"

"And stop that Yes Sir bullshit or I'll have you keel hauled."

"Yes – Ca – Freddy. You want something Sofia?"

"A Sprite if there's one there."

"I'll be right back."

Jade brought up two Sprites and a frosty cold can of Negra Modelo beer with a bag of peanuts. "Where are we headed Cap – Freddy?" she asked handing him his drink.

"Bimini, and some of the best fish chowder you've ever tasted. If we catch a Dorado on the way over, I'll have the restaurant prepare it with their special white wine sauce that's to die for."

They spent the next ten days fishing, gunk-holing, diving and making love. Freddy's video porno collection and sex toys made for lots of experimenting and wondering, how those people in the videos do it.

After the last night ashore and a superb meal they motored out to Mary-Belle in the rubber Zodiac tender earlier than usual. Freddy led them into the main salon where he poured all of them a light port. Lifting his in toast he said, "It's been a good, fun, time. I don't know when I have enjoyed myself more."

They raised their glasses and toasted each other, "To good times and good fortune," Jade responded.

"To good friends," Sofia joined in.

Freddy poured himself another port before shifting into his serious captain's voice, "Sofia, Jade, I have a proposition to offer you, are you interested?"

"What is it? What are you talking about?" Sofia asked.

"I'm talking about marriage and five-million dollars apiece."

"What?" Jade was shocked, "You can't be serious."

Sofia took a big swallow of her port.

"But I am; I've known you long enough to know that while you're working girls, you have class, and a sense of correctness. Lily says you're the best she's ever had. You're not ignorant Bimbos, you show well, and we all love each other. Yup, marriage is a good idea."

"Freddy, this wouldn't work out. Your parents would have a heart attack, if you came home with a Chinese wife." Jade reasoned.

"True; but if I came home with Slovakian royalty they would be impressed."

Sofia was caught off guard, "You mean me? You favor Jade. I don't think..."

"Let me start at the beginning. What I'm about to say comes from a lot of thought. First, while I have a generous living allowance Mother has made it clear unless I marry and settle down, Dad is going to leave his fortune to a charity for homeless puppies – or something. We're talking about a lot of money – a very big lot of money. Now if I marry some broad Mom or Dad has selected, they will demand half in the event of a divorce – and I don't like that idea."

"While I favor you Jade, my dear, old-fashioned Mother is prejudiced; she'll never agree to an Oriental daughter-in-law." Freddy stood up, pulling Jade off the couch he wrapped his arms around her holding and rocking her gently he whispered in her ear, "Jade – love, it's gotta be this way you know."

"I know," she was near tears.

"My sweet little poor Butterfly I love you." He added as they separated.

"However, Mama would accept you Sofia. By the same token, I don't want to break up a set – you two – huh, we three – belong together. So, here's my offer: I will give each of you five-million-dollars based upon Sofia marrying me. Jade will be our live-in companion – a friend of both of us. Sofia, you will sign a pre-nuptial agreement whereby the five-million and like-gift to Jade will suffice in the event of a divorce and you'll make no claim on my inheritance. I'll set it all up with an escrow account; everything will be absolutely on the up-and-up."

Sofia was the first to answer, "Freddy, there's no question ten million dollars is a lot of money; still I think this is something Jade and I will have to talk over in private."

"I agree; why don't you two spend the night in the guest stateroom and give me your answer in the morning?"

Jade chimed in, "Five-million dollars is a lot, but I'll feel like extra baggage, like some kind of tagalong."

Freddy reached over to put his arm around her, "Jade honey, I would marry you if I could, but this is the only way success will be guaranteed. We'll still be the three musketeers."

They finished the wine and went off to separate quarters after sharing a circle hug and kisses. Freddy went aft to the master cabin, the girls forward to the guest stateroom.

Undressing in silence the two climbed into the double bed leaving the nightstand light on. Jade was the first to speak, "What do you think; ten-million is a lot of money."

"True, but he is going to inherit at least over a billion; his father is wealthy beyond belief. I think we are being offered too little."

"Perhaps, but he can always find others who will jump at the opportunity. The interest on ten-million at two-percent is over sixteen thousand a month; we'd never have to turn another trick," Jade reasoned.

"Okay, but I vote for demanding he pay the taxes on the ten million; we want ten net – in cash."

"Agree." Jade reached over to turn out the light and give Ani a kiss goodnight.

"Are you tired?" Sofia asked as she put her arm around Jade.

"A little, but I'm never too tired for you." She responded as she snuggled up to Sofia. "Where did you get that?" Sofie asked.

"From Freddy's toy-chest. Let's play," Jade responded.

The low light barely provided enough for the images on the TV screen in Freddy's stateroom, however the sound was excellent. He was glad he'd installed the hidden system; it more than paid for itself tonight. *I guess I have inherited a bit of my Dad's craftiness,* he mused as he pleasured himself while watching the two images perform, enjoying their little cries of pleasure over the TV monitor.

The next morning after breakfast they presented their counter proposal. He hesitated, appearing concerned, before hesitatingly agreeing to their demand; it amounted to pennies compared to the billion he would inherit. *Life was good*, he thought.

On the return voyage to Fort Lauderdale they landed a twenty-five-pound Dorado. It was prepared and served with a wonderful California Chablis by the marina restaurant for their pleasure. The flight home was another fun run; the autopilot and GPS doing all the work while the three of them enjoyed each other in the cabin.

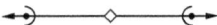

Freddy's mother was thrilled to hear her son had selected a bride. She was even more delighted to discover Sofia was descended from royalty. His father expressed congratulations before alerting the head of his security department to check her out. A date was set for three months away, plenty of time for everyone to get acquainted and run background checks.

Lily was pleased for both of them, although she expressed regrets at losing two such good employees. "Cousin, you've grabbed the golden ring; enjoy it while you can. God has certainly smiled on you both."

Sofia purchased a more conservative wardrobe, charming Mary-Belle with her slight accent, "May I call you Sofia, Princess?"

"Please do, Princess is only a title; to my friends I'm always Sofia."

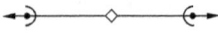

Clarice was indispensable, providing Ani with suggestions on what to wear and how to act and talk. "Always remember you are a

Princess, so be a little aloof. If someone asks you a question you can't answer, blame it on your sheltered upbringing."

Time quickly flew; suddenly there was only a week to go before the wedding. Freddy's father flew out to New York to have lunch with his son in his New York penthouse. The meal was a simple smoked salmon salad with a delicious Chardonnay. Freddy was surprised at how pleasant the conversation with his father was going considering their past antagonisms.

It was during coffee that his Dad turned serious, "Freddy, what do you really know of Sofia?"

"The same thing you know Dad, isn't she a beauty?" Wondering where this was leading.

"She is that –" Frederick Senior put a manila file on the table before continuing, "– and a bit more."

Opening the thick file, he went down the information his security chief had discovered point by point: "Her real name is Ani Vlasicova. Her father and older brother are both dead. Her mother and two older sisters are maids in a Prague hotel..." Frederick Senior continued until he'd finished with, "You met them as high-priced party girls. You've been living with them ever sense. You negotiated an agreement whereby you are going to give them ten-million after tax dollars for agreeing to marry you and not ask for more. What is your reaction to all of this?"

"My first reaction is; Dad, you've got one helluva good security department. My second is; why do you want to know all this shit. She's a good person, who presents herself well and is not going to give me any problems down the line."

"Points well taken; while you will be marrying well below your financial station, you will be marrying someone you can control. Your Mother came from poor stock in Alabama and she's proven to be a great benefit to me. According to my attorney you signed Sofia to a bullet-proof prenup. That was good thinking on your part. Your Mother likes her; she does come across well. My feeling is she may settle you down so you'll be able to do something productive. Now, about this Jade – uh, Clarice; she's estranged from her family, her father's a successful real estate investor in the San Francisco area. She's given birth to four children that she's abandoned. I think that about covers it."

Freddy was surprised to hear about the children and it took him a moment to reply, "Dad she's part of the package. I know it sound weird, but the three of us fit like a tight puzzle." *Four kids? Wow, and she still has a beautiful body. How did she do it?* he thought.

Frederick stared at his son for a few moments before taking another sip of his coffee. "Freddy, you've got the sex-drive of a two-pecker'd-billy-goat; if these women will settle you down, then I'm for it." *I'd rather have a Satyr-maniac for a son than a druggie or alcoholic.* "Good luck and God bless," he said before breaking into a smile. "Let's keep this lunch between us, there's no sense in your mother finding out."

"Yes Dad – thank you – thank you for everything," a relieved Freddy stood up and shook his Dads hand before giving him a hug and kiss on the cheek.

The meeting was over; Sofia and Jade had passed muster.

The wedding took place at the Duponte's Beverly Hills mansion. Their garden was aglow in flowers. Mary-Belle had gone out of her way to make the small affair as perfect as possible. In addition to a few family friends, Lily had arrived in a light, conservative flora printed dress with a big floppy hat looking every bit the charming, successful, female entrepreneur. Jade dressed in pale pink, played her role as bridesmaid perfectly. A reception followed. The society page of the Los Angeles Times printed a few lines, "... eligible bachelor

Frederick Duponte II was no longer available as he'd swept Princess Sofia of Slovakia off her feet. Sorry girls, you had your chance."

Frederick graciously gave them the use of the Gulfstream for the honeymoon. "I'll make-do with the King Air for a month. Don't trash the interior; the lamb skin cost a fortune."

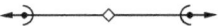

First stop was Claridge's in London. The jet landed at Stanstead where the five-star hotel's limo awaited their arrival. Browsing the art salons of Fleet Street Freddy bought a small oil painting that caught his eye, "Ship it to my Manhattan apartment, please; I don't want to load down the plane with packages. Thanks." The London theatre district offered two plays they all three enjoyed, "Freddy, I'm so glad you like the theatre, they're much better here than Manhattan, don't you think? Jade commented with a smile; adjusting quickly to the benefits of being really rich.

Then, it was off to Lucerne and a ride on the lake, "That's where Julie Andrews and Blake Edwards live," Freddy commented, pointing to a lovely lakeside villa.

"Which did you like better, Vienna or Budapest?"

"Rome has a lot of history, but it's too crowded."

"The coliseum was a trip."

"Sofia, do you want to visit Prague?"

"I don't think so; too many bad memories, thanks anyway."

"How about Athens?"

"I don't think so, too much smog. Let's do Lisbon."

"Okay."

The month went by in a flurry of top-of-the-line hotels, fine dining, and superb sightseeing; with always a limo at their disposal.

Flying home over the Atlantic the formally dressed male steward had just served lunch, "What do you say we ask Dad for the jet next year and do Russia? Saint Petersburg has a killer museum," Freddy asked as he motioned to the attendant to pour more Chardonnay.

"We could do that or tour the South Pacific; have you ever been to Tahiti?" Jade answered extending her glass.

"We could do Croatia; I hear it's got a beautiful coastline." Sofia put in.

"Whatever; I'm sure glad the three of us get along – it's been a swell time, don't you agree?"

"Agree!" they both smilingly responded.

"Do you think we ought to join the Six-Mile-High Club?"

"I think it would be a good way to really piss off your father. You know the crew couldn't keep a secret," Sofia admonished.

"We can join the Three-Mile-High Club twice on your plane and call it the Six-Miles-High Club." Jade reasoned.

"Hell, we could make it the Nine-Mile-High Club that way," Freddy laughed. "To us," he said, raising his glass.

The three lifted their glasses in toast, "To us."

Observing them discreetly from the forward galley the steward thought, *the rich do live differently.* He hoped they'd like the pâté foie he planned for a later snack.

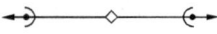

"You two go ahead; I don't care to see men prancing up and down the avenue in tutus."

"Aw come on, it's not all about gay guys. Gay Pride in San Francisco is all about a bunch of fun parties and there's the parade; the Dykes on Trikes are a riot."

"Naw, you both go on; I'm going fishing on the boat."

"Miss us?"

"Terribly; don't go foolin' around on me."

"Never."

Jade and Sofia left the next day on United Airlines for three days in the City by the Bay. Freddy flew down to Fort Lauderdale in the King Air to do some trolling.

The flight out in first class was routine, a luxury suite at the St. Francis comfortable. San Francisco was its usual cold and windy self. Beggars hustled, cable cars clanged, shoppers jostled and tourists gawked. "Growing up in Piedmont, we seldom came over here, it's cold and damp and the locals are loony," Clarice commented as she put on her jacket before venturing out of the hotel.

"My partner, Natalie, and I visited here several times before I went to work for you. She liked it, but I didn't. That's where she left me for a butch dyke. I sometimes wonder what she's doing now; she's probably fat and ugly."

They hopped a cable car to Fisherman's Wharf and dinner at Swiss Louie's before heading back to the hotel. Both were tired from the flight and the time zone change

The king-sized bed had been turned down by the maid, a chocolate rested on each pillow. Clarice was coming out of the bathroom after brushing her teeth. Ani was glancing through a Condé Nast periodical when she mentioned, "Why don't you give your mother a call; maybe set up a lunch. It's been years since you've spoken…"

"Ten – it's been ten years; I was thinking the same thing. I wonder how the kids are doing."

"Give her a call; it's not yet nine o'clock here."

Clarice sat down staring at the phone trying to make up her mind. Finally, picking up the receiver she dialed the number still remembered by heart. After four rings the answering machine came on with Allison's voice, "You have reached the Chan residence. Please leave a message."

"Hello – hello Mom; this is Clar…"

There was a click and scratch, "Clarice? Clarice this is your mother, wait a minute while I shut off the damned answering machine."

There followed a few more clicks until Allison's voice finally came back clearly, "Clarice, where are you? Are you all right?"

"I'm in San Francisco. I'm all right. How's everybody?"

A flood of words poured out over the line. Allison was so happy to hear from her daughter; Clarice relaxed, there was no sound of anger or guilt, just a warm mother's joy at making contact with her only child. After thirty minutes they made a date the next day for lunch near Allison's travel agency in Chinatown. Hanging up, Clarice asked Ani, "Do you mind…"

"Mind? Of course not; you go ahead and have lunch with your Mother. She sounded glad to hear from you. I'm going to do some shopping. See you back here for cocktails?"

"She was. I don't think I've ever heard her so excited and happy. Five o'clock sounds good. I'm tired let's turn in."

"After I brush my teeth; warm a spot for me, will you?"

"I'll try but I may be asleep before you crawl in."

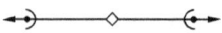

The Jade Villa was a typical Chinese restaurant; all hustle and bustle with great food and lots of noise from the patrons. Clarice was dressed casually in black, tailored pants, a white blouse and jacket. She was a little nervous until she spied her mother's smiling face advancing towards her with arms outstretched.

Big teary hugs followed, "Oh Clarice, I've so worried about you. You can't imagine the worry I've gone through. You look as beautiful as ever; you haven't changed. How do you do it?"

"Mom, I'm so glad to see you; to feel your arms around me. It's been a long time."

"Too long."

Allison ordered enough food to feed six, "You can take it back to the hotel," was the answer to Clarice's protests.

Clarice not wishing to go into details said she was living in New York, still single, but in a relationship that was solid.

Allison told her about Tommy coming down with Alzheimer's disease. "His business is shut down. I've had to put him in a nursing home. I can't cope with him. Half the time he doesn't know who he is."

"I'm sorry to hear that, Dad worked hard to provide for all of us. Can I visit him?"

"He did, but his mind has left, leaving the body behind." Rummaging through her purse she produced a small business card and handed it to Clarice, "Here's the place where your father is located – it's in Berkeley."

"Could you take me there; I don't have a car."

"I'll drop you off, however, I don't like to see your father like he is; it is too distressing. I'm moving back to Hong Kong."

"What? That seems drastic. Why? What about your business?"

"I've sold it to my employees; they will be paying me for the next ten years. There's something I want to tell you. Something I've kept from you and it's time to share."

"What is it?"

"Tommy is not your biological father. I became pregnant by a schoolmate that was not your father. He was from a poor family; my parents did to me what I did to you. They arranged a marriage with the son of an equally successful family. Tommy thought you arrived premature, but actually you were right on schedule. I always thought Fate was playing tricks again."

"My God," Clarice was shocked at her mother's revelation. "Then that's why TC and Charlene were healthy normal babies; there was no incest?

"Yes. Part of my anger at you, was the frustration of you repeating the same mistake I had made seventeen years earlier. The reason I'm going back to Hong Kong is the classmate and I never lost contact; all my trips to China were to spend some time with him."

My God my Mother has been cheating on Dad all this time. Dad and I are not blood related. It could have all been different. "Mom does anyone else know this?"

"No. I'm sharing it with you because of all the time that has passed and I'm getting older…"

"God." Clarice was blown away by her Mother's admission, she wanted to change the subject, "How are the kids, how's TC, and how's Nelson?"

"The children are all healthy, smart, and well behaved. TC has your beauty and her grandfather's personality; she's always smiling, everybody loves her. Andrew and Benjamin take after Nelson; they're more serious and good students. Charlene is not as extroverted as TC, but still beautiful and charming, she'll do well in college.

Nelson is now running his Father's business; he is very successful. He and his wife are active in the church. She had no children; she treats yours as if they were her own. They love her unreservedly.

"That's good, I'm glad to hear Nelson provided a good environment for them."

"Why don't you come over and re-introduce yourself to the children. I know they'd be overjoyed to see their real mother; particularly TC."

"I can't; I feel so bad, so much time has gone by… No, I can't… I need more time."

"Can I tell them I saw you?"

"No. Please leave it like it is. Nelson and his wife have done a fine job; I don't want to do anything to upset that balance."

Two hours went by in a flash. The drive over the Bay Bridge in Allison's Mercedes was breathtaking. They took the University off ramp towards the college. Allison wound through several residential streets before pulling up in front of a clean, single story unassuming building with a small sign on the front lawn identifying it as, Shady Side Rest Home. Pulling up to the curb Clarice promised to keep in touch. There were hugs and tearful goodbyes before she opened the door to walk up the cement path to the entrance.

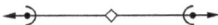

Behind a desk in the clean, neat lobby sat a woman in a white uniform, "May I help you?" she asked as Clarice approached her.

"Yes, I'm Clarice Chan, Tommy Chan's daughter; may I visit him?"

The woman checked a paper on her desk before answering, "He's in room twelve – down the hall on your left. He may be taking his nap."

"If you don't mind, I'll walk down to check."

"That will be fine. Please sign here; we log all our visitors."

Clarice signed in and walked through a set of double doors that opened to a hallway. Several men sat in wheel chairs, staring vacantly ahead. Glancing in the small patient's rooms she noted individuals sleeping. Orderlies scurried about on missions unknown; it was not a happy place.

The door to room twelve was ajar; she pushed it open a bit more to make out a thin old man in light blue hospital shirt and pants staring at a television game show with no sound. His hair was disheveled; his face a blank expression.

"Dad? Dad, it's me, Clarice."

The old man turned slowly to look at her before answering, "What is your name?"

"Clarice."

He looked her up and down, "I had a daughter named Clarice; what's your name?"

"Clarice, Dad." She was looking for a sign of recognition.

"I had a daughter named Clarice; what's your name?"

"Oh Dad," she took his hand; it was cold and limp and unresponsive. "Daddy, it's me; your kitten."

He stared at her for a moment before responding, "I had a daughter named Clarice; what's your name?"

Clarice bent over to kiss his forehead, Tommy continued, "I don't like the sound on the television. What's your name?"

Clarice drew back to look at what was once the love of her life. Tears began to roll down her cheeks. Tommy continued to stare vacantly at the game show, his jaw slack and mouth open.

The two remained together for another five minutes until Clarice bent over to say farewell. "Goodbye, Dad. God Bless."

Tommy slowly turned away from the television to look at her. For just a moment Clarice hoped he recognized her. He spoke in the same tone, "I had a daughter named Clarice; what's your name?"

The woman at the front desk called her a taxi. Clarice realized more than ever; she was on her own as far as family ties were concerned. She would have liked to have seen her Dad one more time, but that was not to be. The man watching the game show was a stranger; it wasn't the man she once knew and loved.

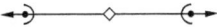

The next day Market Street was crowded with people waiting to see the parade; everyone in a festive holiday mood. Gay rainbow flags waved from every lamp post and were carried by many. Men wore outrageous female costumes; their faces made-up to look over-the-top feminine, a lot of them sported long haired wigs; they looked like something out of a grotesque, surreal fantasy movie. The women for the most part were more conservative with only a minority of husky, tattooed, mean looking butches. Body piercing and art were common among the spectators.

The floats featured a variety of dancers of both sexes in every imaginable costume. There were Tahitian tamure, Hawaiian hula, Brazilian Bosa-nova, and bump & grind boob-flashing performers all smiling, laughing and enjoying the event as much as the spectators. Foot tapping music by top quality musicians intermingled with the floats playing jazz, reggae, marching, and everything in between.

"This is fun; have you ever seen so many Gays in one place?" Clarice asked Ani between bites of popcorn.

"No, San Francisco Gays certainly know how to throw a party."

"I'm having a good time; what do you think about getting a tattoo?" Clarice blurted out.

"What?"

"I mean like maybe a small bee on the butt, or a rose, or something…"

"It would sure surprise Freddy…" Ani thoughtfully responded.

"Let's do it – we each get one and surprise Freddy."

"Let me think about it. It would have to be a clean shop; I'd hate to get an infection. Oh, here come the Dykes on Trikes."

A loud roar of Harleys echoed off the buildings as a hundred, five abreast barking and snorting Harley Davison motorcycles slowly made their way up Market Street. Driving the beasts were strong, masculine looking females wearing black leather chaps, helmets, and tops that showed off their body painting and piercings. Most carried a good-looking female passenger behind them who waved and smiled at the crowd, their long hair flying in the breeze. Tattooed arms and backs looked a lot like something out of a carnival.

"The noise is hurting my ears," Clarice said as she handed Ani the popcorn bag and covered her ears with her hands.

"They are loud. I'm looking for Natalie; she ditched me for one of those pigs. - Look -"

"Look – look there; the third bike in – the black one with the chrome and red trim. That's her – see?"

"I don't – yes – yes, I see; is she the one wearing the lace top with the tattooed boobs?"

"Yeah, that's her. God, she's covered in tattoos and look at that – she's wearing a nose ring."

The Harley was driven by a two hundred pounder in dark sun glasses staring straight ahead with a cigar clamped between her lips. The girl behind her was laughing and waving at the crowd with one hand, and holding onto the back of the driver's chaps with the other. They slowly passed by.

"Aren't you going to yell a hello to her?" Clarice asked.

"No, why should I; she left me, I didn't leave her. I hope she got what she wanted, whatever that is. Oh, here comes a Samba group."

After the parade they gravitated with the crowd toward Castro Street which was packed with revelers. They were fortunate to find a small table in a restaurant that served a good seafood salad with a chilled Sauvignon Blanc.

"Wow, the place is packed; it's good to sit down." Clarice said as she reached for her napkin.

"I think there are more Gays in San Francisco than anywhere else in the World. Check out the two guys kissing in the corner; he's stroking his partner's dick under his jeans."

"I saw it; and, they're all here today. It is a lot of fun and I do enjoy seeing and being with all these people, but I like the way we live better, don't you?" Clarice continued, as she took a sip from the cold long-stemmed glass.

"I do too; this over-the-top display of public sexuality isn't for me. It's funny; you and me have lived a life of sex, and we're living an unusual lifestyle today, but I prefer a more modest public display. Do you think we're finally growing up?"

"We're not even close to growing up. I think we're just more conservative. Good wine, huh?"

"I love California wine; even the cheap stuff is good."

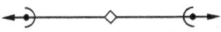

Arriving back home, they couldn't wait to show Freddy their new tattoos. Jade bared her butt to display a small butterfly on the left cheek.

"Like it?" she saucily asked as she wiggled.

"Love it; and I like the tattoo." Freddy jokingly responded as he gave her a light slap on the art work.

"Check this out," Sofia said as she exposed a rose just above and to the right of her pussy.

"Looking up close Freddy took in a deep breath, saying, "I can even smell it."

They were all glad to be back together as a team. Freddy opened a bottle of Dom Perignon to celebrate.

"To us – The Three Musketeers," he announced.

"To us," the two responded in unison.

"Are tattoos all you brought back from the City by the Bay?"

"If you mean what I think you mean, that's all we brought back; we were good girls."

"Yup, beside those people out there are all weird. We saw more tattoos and piercings than you'd find at the circus. What about you; did you fuck any Miami hookers on Mary-Belle?"

"No as a matter of fact I stayed straight. Estefan, the dock boy, and I went fishing. I caught two Dorado and he got a beautiful Snapper which we barbequed for dinner. In addition to taking care of the boats, Estefan is a damned fine cook."

"What did you do with the Dorados?" Jade asked.

"I gave them to the restaurant in exchange for dinners."

"Sounds like a good trade," Sofia added.

"It was; Estefan and I dined. He was happy to get away from the dock and I was glad to have the company. Did you eat on the plane?"

"We snacked, airplane food doesn't taste good," Sofia answered.

"I'll bet you're both tired; how about a light dinner and early to bed?" Freddy inquired.

"Sounds good to me," Jade confirmed.

"Me too, let's all shower before turning in. I could use some hot water pounding on my poor, tired, body." Sofia put in.

"And, maybe a rub down?" Jade perked up.

"Maybe," Sofia answered with a come-hither smile.

"I'll have Mario fix us a light dinner," Freddy added.

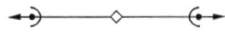

A month passed when over breakfast Freddy complained of a cold, "I feel like shit; I think I'm coming down with something."

"Why don't you make an appointment with Doctor Feelgood, he can probably prescribe you something." Sofia replied."

"I'll call him; he costs a fortune for a visit." Freddy excused himself and went into the Library to use the phone.

Returning a few minutes later, Sofia Asked, "What did he say?"

"He said it was probably a virus that's going around and there's nothing he can do – there's no cure for a virus – he said take aspirin and drink lots of water. The damned thing should clear up in three to seven days."

A week later Freddy still was feeling lousy; he had a sore throat and diarrhea. "I'm going down to see that quack there's got to be something he can prescribed to get rid of this crap," he grumpily commented to the girls.

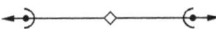

"You do look like the devil, Freddy; how long have you had this?" the doctor asked.

"It's been over a week Doc; can't you give me some antibiotic? Maybe I've got an infection."

The doctor stuck a thermometer in Freddy's mouth and took his blood pressure. "Get on the scales, let's see what you weigh, Freddy."

"Humm, one fifty-three; that's a little under your last visit; you were one fifty-nine back then." He removed the thermometer, saying, "You are running a little fever…"

"I haven't been eating well since I got this damned cold. Yeah, and I've got a sore throat."

"I'm going to prescribe some antibiotic; that should knock out whatever you've got."

But it didn't; a month went by and Freddy continued to feel poorly. The anti-biotic had no effect; the fever persisted, and he began having night sweats. The girls moved into the guest bedroom.

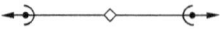

"Doc, you've got to do something; I feel absolutely terrible."

"I thought that drug would clear you up. Does this hurt?" he said pressing on a lymph gland."

"Ouch, yes – yes it does – what's that mean?"

"I'm going to draw some blood and I want you to give me a sample of your urine. I'm going to run some tests before we shotgun anything else. Hold still."

Three days later Jade was watching her favorite soap opera when the phone rang. She let it go to the answering machine.

The receptionist's professional voice announced, "This is Doctor Shapiro's office calling for Mister Duponte. The Doctor wants to see you as soon as possible."

Jade waited for the commercial to get up and see if Freddy was awake. *This bug has really got him down. He sleeps all the time.* Opening the bedroom door a crack, she peaked in.

"I heard the phone ring; who was it?" he sleepily asked.

"Doctor Shapiro's office; they want to see you."

"What did you tell them?"

"I let it go to the answering machine. The voice sounded urgent."

"Christ, I better give them a call; he's probably got the results of all that blood he sucked out of me. Oh damn – I gotta shit – oh damn…" he struggled out of bed making a beeline for the toilet.

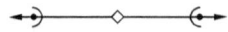

"Yes, I have the results from the tests. Sit down Freddy; I'm afraid I have some bad news for you." Doctor Shapiro had lowered his voice an octave, assuming his most serious professional manner.

Sitting down on the edge of the examining table Freddy countered, "What is it, Doc? What did the tests show? What have I got?"

Doctor Shapiro reached out, putting his hand on Freddy's shoulder, in a softer, kinder voice he began, "This isn't going to be easy... I don't know any other way to put it ... Freddy – Fred, you've got AIDS/alpha-two..."

Freddy was shocked into disbelief, "That's impossible! Something's wrong - they mixed up the tests..."

"They didn't mix up the tests. When the lab gave me the results, I called the head of the department and he confirmed the diagnosis. Something this serious always requires the senior lab technician's confirmation. You have AIDS/alpha-two now, do you know where you got it?"

"I don't know – I don't... What is AIDS anyway?"

"AIDs is an acronym for, Acquired Immune Deficiency; it is a virus that attacks a person's immune system making it impossible for the individual to fight off other lesser viral infections. A cold could lead to pneumonia and death. A sore throat could morph into a kidney infection and death. Although it's normally a disease transmitted by homosexuals, it is found in a minority of cases through heterosexual contacts. Could you have acquired it from either Sofia or that other girl you live with? Is it possible they could have infected you?"

"No – no I don't think so. They did go out to California a month ago, but they said they didn't do anything..."

"Well, I think you'd better have them make an appointment to see me. They may have given it to you; or you may have infected them. Have you been with anyone other than those two?"

"No, – no, just them." Then, it hit him: Estefan, the Brazilian dock boy!

"All my friends call me Estefani; you'll be gentle, won't you?" That sonofabitch! He said he never fooled around. I paid him two hundred dollars – to get AIDS – Jesus! Oh God, how am I going to tell Sofia and Jade? What am I going to say to Mom and Dad?

"I'll bring them in; give me a few days," Freddy continued in shock.

"Don't wait too long; have they showed any of the signs you have?"

"No, I don't think so – they both look healthy"

"Not every one that's infected has the severe reaction you have. Get them here as soon as you can. I'm sorry…"

"Isn't there anything you can do?"

The pharmaceutical industry is working around the clock to arrive at a cure for the Alpha-Two retrograde as fast as they can, but so far nothing has been successful… You never know; maybe tomorrow."

"Yeah, maybe tomorrow. How long do I have?"

"It varies; could be a year – it could be ten."

Whew – do you have anything for a headache?"

"Go down to the pharmacy, I'll have them prescribe something strong. Do you want anything to make you sleep?"

"I sleep a lot, but not well. Yeah, maybe that would be a good idea." Freddy shakily stood up and shook hands with the doctor, "Wow, thanks for your time. I wish you had better news. Oh, you'd better sterilize the hand I just shook."

"Son, I wish I did too – you don't get AIDS from handshakes. God speed."

There was a cocktail lounge a half a block from the medical building, Freddy walked in to the dimly lit room stumbling over a chair on the way to the bar.

"What'll it be?" the old bartender asked as he wiped the spot in front of Freddy and threw down a napkin.

"Dewar's rocks – make it a double," Freddy answered as he reached into his pocket for the headache pills. "Oh, and let me have a glass of water, no ice, please."

The two brown plastic bottles were identical in shape and size; the headache capsules were blue; the sleeping drugs, yellow. He quickly downed two blues, his head was exploding.

One stupid weekend; – one stupid fucking weekend was all it took for a death sentence… It isn't fair; why me God? – I know damned well I've infected Sofia – and Jade… Mom's going to cry; Dad's going to tell me he knew something like this would happen… I oughta kill that fucking Estefani… It's all the fault of that damned English boarding school… Everybody did it…If they'd have let us have girls… Aw fuck… How am I going to break the news to Mario?

"Bartender, pour me another one."

"Yes sir; that one went down fast, you okay?"

"I got a headache; I'll be all right."

The doorman called Mario, who came down to help Freddy up the elevator; he was drunk out of his mind. "I'm okay – I'm okay; I can make it," he said as he bounced off the wall and stumbled into the living room.

"Jade looked up from the television shocked at the apparition, "Freddy, you're smashed! God, I've never seen you so drunk."

"I'm okay I tell you," he wheezed.

She got up, quickly advancing towards the two men, "Mario, take him into the bedroom; I'll give you a hand…"

"I gotta poop – I gotta shit. I'm okay – take me to the bathroom – oh fuck…" Freddy soiled his pants.

"Mario, help me get him undressed and showered off. I've never seen him this drunk. Could he be on drugs?'

"I don't think so, Freddy doesn't do drugs,"

Going through his pants Mario found the two bottles of medicine; both had warning labels not to be taken with liquor. "This might be it; if he took one of these with some booze it gave him a reaction."

"Help me get him to bed. When did Sofia say she was coming back?"

"She's been gone a couple of hours; it should be anytime."

"I don't know what to do; should we call the doctor."

"I don't think so; just let him sleep it off. I'm sure he'll be all right, Jade. I'll put off my shopping until Sofia returns."

"Thanks, I wouldn't know what to do if he needed help."

The next morning Freddy joined them for breakfast looking awful; his hair a mess, eyes all blood-shot, he hadn't shaved "Wow, I feel terrible; I wonder if that bartender slipped me a Mickey? Pour me a cup of coffee, will you? Thanks."

"Mario said he thought you mixed booze and those headache pills he found in your pants. How did you sleep?" Jade replied as she poured him a cup.

"I was knocked out; the sheets are wet with sweat…"

"What did the doctor say about your illness?' Sofia asked.

"He said I had a virus and it would just have to take its course…"

"Can't he give you some antibiotics?"

"No, they only work on bacterial infections; there's no drug for a virus infection. That's why they can't cure a cold." Shakily, he took a long, noisy, sip of coffee. "Are you guys all right? Doc said what I had might be contagious."

"We're okay I think," Jade answered. "Sofia didn't you say you had a sore throat the other day?"

"Yes, but I took some lozenges and I think it's gone away."

"You know what I'm thinking? I'm thinking why don't we take a run down to Miami and go to Bimini on Mary-Belle like we did last year?"

"Are you all right to fly?" Sofia worried.

"I'm okay; maybe the altitude and change of climate will do me good. Let's plan on leaving Monday, that'll give us five days to pack, plus there's less air traffic during the week days. I'll call the marina and have them get Mary-Belle ready." *I'll break the news to them on Mary-Belle; they can't have AIDS... Maybe Estefani doesn't know he's got AIDS, I've gotta let him know. I'm sure the dumb shit doesn't want to infect the whole marina.*

"I wouldn't mind; fresh Dorado and a change in climate might be just what you need." Jade worriedly agreed.

"We can put off Saint Petersburg until after you get better," Sofia concurred.

"Oh – you two are going to have to stay in the guest bedroom. The Doc said no more close contact until after I get over this virus. Sorry,"

Jade leaned over to give him a hug and a kiss. Freddy dodged the kiss and took the hug, "Hugs are okay, but no kissy-face; I don't want you getting what I got."

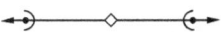

Climbing in the plane Jade followed Freddy up the boarding ladder, "You have lost weight; your uniform shirt fits you like it was made for someone else."

"Yeah, I know; I've gotta start eating more," Freddy replied as he headed forward to the cockpit; the headache made it hard to concentrate on the normal preflight checklist he performed before starting the engines. Turning around to the cabin he caught Sofia's eye, "Honey, will you get me two of those pills in the brown bottle in my shaving bag; my damned head is pounding."

"Sure; are you going to be all right to fly?" Sofia answered with a worried expression as she walked to the back of the plane to dig out his shaving kit from the overnight bag.

"I'll be okay as soon as we get in the air and away from all this traffic and radio noise."

What traffic and what noise? Sofia wondered as she tapped out two yellow capsules from one of the brown bottles and poured a paper cup three-quarter full of water from the galley. *That damned virus sure is making him act strange sometimes.* "Here," she said putting the two pills in his hand.

Freddy popped them into his mouth without bothering to look at them and reached for the water, washing down the pills in two big gulps. "Wow, I hope they kick in soon; my head is going to explode." Handing the empty cup back to Sofia he saw the worried expression and tried to comfort her, "Don't worry, I'll be alright; the autopilot's going to do all the work once we get in the air. Did you pack in the tuna sandwiches?"

"Mario gave us tuna, roast beef and some pastrami with Swiss; do you want one now?"

"No, I'll eat after we get leveled off, I was just checking."

Completing the checklists Freddy started the Pratt & Whitney turbines and taxied out for takeoff. He hadn't filed the recommended FAA flight plan; he and the plane knew the route by heart. Besides, he didn't want to be bothered talking to air traffic controllers on the radio. The takeoff was normal; he engaged the autopilot at fifteen hundred feet climbing to eleven thousand-five hundred feet, the correct altitude for his direction of flight. Leveling off, he connected the GPS to the autopilot with the programed route he had designed.

Making sure everything was in order and stabilized; he unfastened his safety belt and somewhat clumsily backed out of his seat to the cabin where he sat down on the couch. Unnoticed, he had nudged the vertical speed controller out of its detent for level flight; the plane started an imperceptible descent of two-hundred feet per minute.

Sofia and Jade were facing each other at the table playing a game of poker, using tooth picks for chips.

"Boy, I'm tired; do me a favor and wake me up in a couple of hours. I can't keep my eyes open," Freddy muttered as he stretched out on the divan; his eyelids were closed before his head came to rest on the padded arm.

Sofia glanced over at Freddy's prone form, already snoring slightly, "I'm worried about Freddy; this virus really has him down."

"Yes, and I think I might be coming down with something; this morning I wasn't feeling up to par and I have a small fever," Jade commented as she laid down three aces and swept a pile of toothpicks over to her side.

"My throat is still sore, those lozenges helped a little, but it hurts in the morning. I hope we haven't caught what he's got," Sofia added as she passed Jade the deck for shuffling. "Wait a minute, I'm going to set the alarm; I don't want Freddy to oversleep. We'd play hell landing the plane on our own," she laughed light-heartedly.

Opening a drawer in the galley Sofia dug out a small, mechanical timer and cranked in two hours. She noticed a plastic sandwich bag with a three of brownies in it. "Look what Mario prepared for us." Sofia said as she brought out the bag with the timer.

"Magic Brownies! That Mario is a sweetie; I love the sprinkle of hash he mixes in, not too much – just enough."

"Me too."

"He must have put them there when he stowed the catering. I'll split one with you."

"Good idea; playing poker is a boring way to pass the time. Let's munch one with ice cream."

"Good idea."

Fifty-eight minutes later all on board were asleep when it happened. At 274mph the spinning propellers made contact with the water savagely burying the nose into the low Atlantic swell. The plane flipped on its back with such a violent motion the wings separated from the fuselage. The occupants were killed instantly.

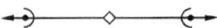

It was days later when a commercial fisherman noticed something reflecting the sun's rays off his starboard beam. Motoring over he saw what looked like an airplane wing bobbing a few feet above the surface. He threw a line around the metal object securing it to a cleat on his boat before calling the Coast Guard and alerting them to what he'd found.

The mystery of what happened to the plane carrying Frederick Duponte II, his wife, Sofia, and their companion Jade, was solved.

The newspapers gave it little notice other than to comment Mr. Duponte was heir to a fortune made by his father. Frederick Duponte Senior saw to it Freddy's assets were returned to the family trust. His mother was heart- broken in grief, "He was just getting his life turned around," she muttered over-and-over to all who'd listen.

Three hotel maids in Prague received checks in the amount of $1,666,666 US dollars each. There was no note or explanation, just a card with, Love, Ani printed on the inside.

Nelson Wong opened a UPS envelope with four certified checks made out in the amount of $1,250,000 each and a letter. It was from

Clarice, instructing him to set up individual accounts for each of the children. The money was to be invested in conservative, interest-bearing, Blue-Chip stocks until each child required it for college. In the event a child chose not to attend college, the total sum in the account was to be turned over to that individual on their thirtieth birthday.

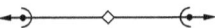

By the time Mario realized he had the dreaded disease he had passed it to ten others who in-turn furthered the spread. Freddie's week of fishing and frolic in Miami resulted in a fatal collateral damage to over six hundred unsuspecting souls.

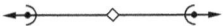

On his morning rounds the Harbormaster spotted Estafan floating face down in a vacant slip. The Coroner ruled the death, Accidental Drowning; he ignored the broken bones in the neck and lack of water in the lungs. *I've already got too much to do with this butt-humping-faggot-caused epidemic to worry about some little Spic that probably got what he deserved,* he thought as he filled out the form that went to Harriet, his secretary to complete the Death Certificate. "I'm going to lunch and the bank; I'll be back about two o'clock if anybody calls," he said as he headed out the door.

END

www.ingramcontent.com/pod-product-compliance
Lightning Source LLC
LaVergne TN
LVHW011729060526
838200LV00051B/3099